The Perfect Woman

LIBBY HALL

Harlequin Books

TORONTO • NEW YORK • LONDON
AMSTERDAM • PARIS • SYDNEY • HAMBURG
STOCKHOLM • ATHENS • TOKYO • MILAN

For Rick, my favorite bachelor,
who tries to answer
all the questions truthfully.

Published February 1988

ISBN 0-373-25289-7

Printed in U.S.A.

1

SHE WAS GIVING orders like a general executing a battle plan.

Sean Stevenson stepped away from the entrance door and the display cases that held the latest editions of Kim Troussard's fashions. He leaned against a wall of pink marble that felt cool and welcoming to his tired back. For several minutes he watched the activity inside the expensive boutique.

Kim Troussard was just as he remembered her—dynamic and aggressive, a bundle of flying energy in a boxy suit of some misty, heathery color of blue. He frowned in irritation at the contrast she presented, feeling he had never quite grasped the essence of her as a person.

Her hair was dark, not quite black but not quite brown, either. It was another of the enigmas about her, for it flew around her shoulders in a rich, luxuriant swirl of curls that didn't go with the image of the General or the successful business tycoon he knew her to be.

Hair like that should belong to a soft, gentle woman, a woman who was gracious and kind and considerate of others....

"Move that stand over! Over there! Not there, over toward the mannequin!" Kim dashed over and grabbed hold of the round stand that was banked with ferns to form a backdrop to a group of gracefully posed dummies and showed the two men exactly where she wanted it placed.

A woman with a voice like silver who could also bellow like a drill sergeant, Sean noted sardonically, one brow lifting in amusement.

A voice like that should be used only in laughter and in loving banter...and in small breathless moans when her man made love to her. Ha! He doubted any man had made love to that tornado in skirts. With her, lovemaking would be a battle of the sexes with the bed serving as the battleground. She would undoubtedly give orders the entire time.

Thinking of her in relation to making love brought an immediate response from his body in spite of his fatigue. That was another thing that irritated him about her—every single time he had seen her, he had wanted her!

They had met at the home of mutual friends, Mary and Martin Holden, a couple of years ago and had seen each other at Mary and Martin's place two or three times a year since, usually at weekend house parties.

As Kim bent from the waist to adjust the line on a taffeta evening skirt, he caught a glimpse of a perfectly proportioned leg—slender ankle, shapely calf and an incredibly beautiful thigh that looked as smooth as the marble he leaned against. Except her flesh would be warm and firm instead of cool and hard. He knew because he had kissed her under the mistletoe once at Mary's laughing insistence.

For a minute a pulse of passion beat through his lower body before he subdued it. He really was exhausted from the long trip if he could get excited over merely a glimpse of thigh on a woman he wasn't sure he even liked. Not that he disliked her, not really. She just wasn't his type of woman.

Perhaps it was the loneliness.

The thought crept into his consciousness, catching him off guard. What else did he want? he questioned irritably. He had several successful businesses going, money enough to live where and how he wished, no ties to slow him down. He compared his life to Martin's. Martin was also successful in business. In addition, he had a settled home, complete with a noisy son and a frisky dog. And he had Mary.

Now *there* was a woman. Soft, shapely, caring. Laughter in her eyes—she could be a little devil of a tease at times—and a smile on her lips. She showered warmth and human kindness on everyone she met.

Naturally she wasn't perfect, but who would want a perfect woman? A woman *should* have some quirks, some odd bits of temperament to go with her feminine mystique and add some unpredictability to the relationship. And she should always be soft-spoken.

Not like the General there. She was yelling at some poor slob to "get the lead out of your behind." Genteel language for a lady who owned one of the country's leading boutique chains of high fashion clothing and her own design house!

Well, he had a job to do here. He might as well get it over with. He pushed himself from the wall with a weary shrug of his massive shoulders.

KIM BURST INTO LAUGHTER when two harried clerks ran into one another, each dropping a tray of jewelry. Everyone around her stopped and laughed, too. Then they helped pick up the stuff and sort it out and put it back in place. A good group.

She experienced a rush of almost maternal love and tenderness for everyone who had helped on this project.

They were all tired, rushed and mentally burned-out, but they were also proud of their accomplishment. They had worked so hard during the past year to make this a reality, and now they were settling into their new offices. The elegant salon on the ground floor opened onto Fifth Avenue. Kim Troussard, Fifth Avenue—wow! She had to grin at her own amazement.

Next week would be the acid test—Grand Opening Day. The press and her invited guests would be admitted to the showroom when she presented her newest collection of high fashion wear. Ten years of work, of eighteen-hour days and sleepless nights, of living on nerves and dreams, had paid off. She was exactly where she had planned to be all those years ago when she had started.

Her one disappointment was that her mom and her best friends, Mary and Martin, who had talked their families and friends into loaning her the money for the new venture, couldn't be present. Mary and Martin were expecting their second child, and her mother was off on a world cruise.

Nor would her father be present. He had died before she had made it to the top, but he had seen the early successes and been proud of her. He had been the one person whose approval she had actively desired, and he had given it, albeit somewhat cautiously. He hadn't been too sure about designing clothing for a living—seemed kind of faddish and uncertain to him, he had told her—and refused to help her out financially at first. But in the end he had come around.

She smiled nostalgically as she glanced at her watch. Darn, she was late. But then, she was always late these days. There just weren't enough hours in the day.

She wheeled about, a slender storm in heather blue, and dashed for the door. With a spine-jarring crash, she ran into . . .

. . . a living mountain, she thought, pushing herself off the massive chest that was clothed in a conservative gray suit jacket. A volcano, she corrected silently, staring up at flaming red hair and a pair of blue-green eyes that made her want to jump into them and drown.

"Good grief," she said, stunned.

"Hello, Kim," Sean acknowledged her recognition of him. "Going to a fire?"

He sounded friendly enough, but Kim intuitively knew he was irritated. For some reason she always brought out his less gentle nature, although with other women he was as gentle as a cat with new kittens. Not that he had ever been less than courteous, she admitted.

"Hello, Sean. What brings you from France—or was it Australia this time?—to the jungles of New York?"

Actually, she wasn't sure where he called home. He was Australian by birth, but he had vineyards in France, an import business here in New York with Martin, plus a ranch in Australia. He spent a lot of time traveling between the three countries.

"First a wine fair at Lake Placid yesterday. That's taken care of. That leaves you as the second order of business."

She thought his tone sounded rather resigned, as if he had fought his fate but had finally given in to performing some unpleasant deed. Her hackles rose. They had a tendency to do so around him, she had discovered. A smile flitted around her mouth at that understatement.

"Why so?" She glanced at her watch again.

Sean felt his irritation flame into anger at her obvious impatience. So she had no time for him, had she? "My Aunt Mattie asked me to get in touch with you."

Kim looked thoroughly puzzled. "Your Aunt Mattie?"

She had never heard of the woman. At least she didn't think she had. Unless she had met her at Mary and Martin's house. Perhaps on one of her visits there.... No, she was very good with names, and she didn't recall an Aunt Mattie.

"She wants to stage a fashion show to introduce the new boutique section in her department stores. Your sports line is one of her featured items. The proceeds will go to charity."

Kim followed his brief explanation. She had recently introduced a mass-production line of casual clothes that would be carried at the "better" department stores.

She smiled brightly. "Please thank her for me, but I'm swamped with work at the moment—"

"She wants you to organize the show and present your spring collection," he continued as if she hadn't spoken. "It would be a wonderful opportunity to introduce your KT Casuals to the Australian market."

"I'm terribly sorry... To where? What Australian market?" she spluttered in surprise.

"The one Aunt Mattie thinks you should get into," he answered calmly.

He looked pleased with himself, as if he had said everything he came to say and could consider his trip a success now that he'd gotten the distasteful task out of the way, she thought, finding herself becoming irritated at his manner. As usual.

For some reason, whenever they had met at Mary's, they had always rubbed each other the wrong way.

Well, she could handle that. She was not of the opinion that everyone had to like her. In fact, she had discovered quite a few men did not. Understanding enough to realize she made them feel insecure, she went on her way with a cheerful, businesslike attitude that soon won her critics all around. Except this one.

"Are her stores in Australia?" she asked.

"Of course."

"Then it looks as if she's opening that market for me. Tell her I said thanks very much! Ask her to drop me a line and let me know how business is going. I'll try to plan a trip down there. Someday."

She was backing toward the exit as she spoke. When she turned to leave, Sean was in front of her before she could reach the door, determinedly blocking the way. Her eyes went to the ormolu clock sitting on a small round table. Late!

"Just a minute—" he began.

"Sean, I really have to—" she started in exasperation.

"We need to talk. Where can we go for lunch?"

"I *have* a luncheon engagement. Which I am late for at this very minute. It was nice seeing you," she added, trying to move him aside. It was like trying to move a granite boulder by speaking nicely to it. The boulder didn't budge.

"Then dinner." He smiled suddenly, and it was so charming that she forgot her irritation and stared up at him.

He was an incredibly handsome man, she realized, as if for the very first time. The other women in the salon weren't so slow on the uptake. Several of them were giving him very friendly smiles.

Kim's glance was enough to send them hurrying about their tasks, then she looked back at Sean. "The volcano," she murmured, a wry smile flickering across her mouth.

"What?" he demanded, frowning again.

"You're like a volcano, huge and flaming, with a threat of violence that you keep carefully hidden beneath those dignified suits you wear." Her eyes filled with laughter.

One brow rose sardonically. "Are you afraid I'll erupt on you, General?"

A tilt at the corners of her mouth was the only acknowledgment she gave of his nickname for her. "Very."

He laughed aloud at this claim, which he knew to be totally false. "Dinner?"

"I really can't," she apologized.

"When may I have a chance to use my persuasive charms on you?" he asked, his voice becoming seductively deep and his lids narrowing sexily over those fascinating eyes.

Kim frowned slightly. He seemed to be enjoying himself while he issued a challenge she didn't quite understand. As was her way, she quickly made a decision and acted on it.

"Tell you what, come to my place tonight. I'm having a cocktail party. Perhaps I can squeeze some time in for you. Here's my card."

She gave him her personal card, which contained her home address and telephone number. As she dashed around him and on her way, she glanced back once. He was watching her out of those mysterious aqua eyes that made her think of tropical waters and faraway places. She smiled and waved. He waved back. Why *had* she invited him to the party at her apartment?

WAS IT TO SHOW him up as a gauche "outback" buckaroo before her highly educated city friends? she questioned as she let herself into her five-room triplex in one of those refurbished brownstone neighborhoods that were home to many of the city's young professionals. A successful commercial artist and an account executive for a public relations firm occupied the other two units in the building.

No, she mused, looking over the accumulation of mail. She had seen Sean Stevenson perfectly at ease with some of the world's wealthiest and most influential people at Mary and Martin's weekend parties. Money was no big thing with him. His father owned one of the largest cattle and sheep stations in Australia. Apparently his Aunt Mattie was quite successful with her department stores, and of course Sean himself had earned his own fortune.

Ever honest with herself, Kim wondered if perhaps she wanted him to see her in a social setting in which she was obviously considered a desirable female by some of New York's most eligible and attractive bachelors.

Crossing the Mexican tiles of the foyer, she stopped in the middle of her living room, trying to see it as an outsider might.

It reflected her interests and something of her inner spirit. She loved fabric and textures, so the walls were hung with tapestries, some original but most copies of old-world designs. Swaths of airy lace crisscrossed the ten-foot-high windows, letting in the bright autumn sky. On one wall was a fireplace stocked with logs, ready for winter's chilling blast.

Although she had been born and raised in New York, she loved the light of the desert and the mountains—sunlight on sand or snow, the air so crystal it made her chest ache just to breathe it. She had tried to capture the feeling in the warm sand tones of the walls and carpets.

And everywhere were ferns and cacti, those hardy survivors of forest floor and desert wasteland. She identified with survivors.

Going into the study, which was characterized by butter-soft, nutty-brown leather and African batiks and carvings, she tossed the mail on the desk, then hurried into her bedroom to shower and change.

The huge shower enclosure was big enough for a man of Sean's proportions, she noted wryly as she stepped inside. That thought sent a frisson down her spine. She considered anew her mixed emotions toward him. What was it about the man that bothered her? Why did she have a need to show him that other men liked her?

She was still very vulnerable in some ways, she admitted. At thirty-one she should have gotten over her need for male approval. Of course, it had only been her father's approval she had ever needed—and now Sean

Stevenson's, for some reason she couldn't discern. What linked the two men in her mind? she wondered. She had loved her father and naturally wanted his blessing, but why did she feel she had to prove anything to that mountain of a man?

Tears filled her eyes, shocking her. Heavens, but she was shaky tonight. She couldn't remember the last time she had been so emotionally off center. It was probably just nerves because of the store opening and the upcoming show.

Finishing her shower, she wrapped a towel around her hair and dried herself off with quick swipes. At five-seven she was tall enough to be a model, but her figure was too curvy. She had to be careful with her weight or she could easily slide into the plumpness that had plagued her as a teenager. As a result her clothing designs tended to have slenderizing lines. Maybe that was why they had caught on with other women so rapidly.

She dressed quickly in a flowing caftan that had the same heathery blue tones she loved to wear. After blowing her hair dry and setting it on large rollers, she applied her makeup with a deft touch. Finished with her face, she brushed out the curls lightly and left them falling onto her shoulders in a dark cloud.

A few minutes later she was in the kitchen talking to Layna, who was preparing the trays of snacks that would be placed on the natural-pine trestle table in the dining room.

"I'll set up the bar," she decided, "since you have everything under control in here."

"The Perrier is in the fridge," Layna advised. She was the wife of a junior accountant and liked to earn extra money by catering the food at small parties, such as this one.

"Oh, good. I meant to do that this morning before I left and forgot." Kim smiled her thanks and went through the swinging door into the dining room.

An antique dry sink served as the bar, and Kim placed a selection of wine on it along with slices of lemon and lime. She centered a large bowl on the polished wood to hold ice and the bottles of mineral water. Pitchers of wine punch would be added later. Since she served no other liquors, cocktail party was a misnomer for her get-togethers, but her guests never complained. The doorbell chimed, and she went to answer.

"Hello, you're early," she said, opening the door so Sean could come inside.

"You didn't say what time," he reminded her.

He was dressed in a dark blue suit with a sweater vest underneath the jacket. It added a friendlier tone to his commanding height and breadth.

"Seven o'clock. It's only six-thirty."

"Good. That gives me thirty minutes to charm your pants off," he joked, giving her a glance that dared her to answer his blatant male-to-female challenge.

He reached out and touched her hair, catching a curl that lay near her breast in his large hand. She experienced a wild, startling sensation, like electricity in the air just before lightning strikes. He released the curl abruptly, dropping his hand to his side and closing it into a fist. The teasing left his eyes, and his expression became unreadable.

She tilted her head to look up at him in a partly saucy, partly thoughtful manner. "I thought you wanted to talk me into going to Australia."

"Maybe I can do both," he suggested. His smile was solemn, for he was no longer sure he was joking. Nor was he sure what had prompted the urge to provoke her in the first place.

Kim studied this new Sean, a man who was not overly large by football-team standards, although he seemed to tower above her like the Rocky Mountains over the western plain. He was perhaps four inches over six feet. For a moment he had looked at her as if she was a woman he found interesting. Should she accept the brief challenge he had offered?

His red hair gleamed like a new penny under the light, and his eyes were the same shade she had seen in a sky at sunset once upon a time. A tightening in her chest brought her hand to her throat. She really was emotionally shaky tonight. What was wrong with her? Handsome men were no rarity in her life. After all, this was New York, a major center of international finance and trade. Eligible males swarmed here to make their fortunes.

"Have a seat." She motioned toward the sofa, noting that one of the colors in the nubby fabric was also the clear blue green of his eyes. She sank into a nearby chair with an unconscious sigh. He remained standing.

"Hard day?" he asked.

She glanced at him, one brow raised in question.

"You sighed. I thought maybe you had had an extra hard day," he explained.

"Oh. No. That is, no harder than the last three hundred or so have been." She grinned at him, suddenly finding the conversation amusing.

He looked around the room and through the open doorways into the others with no self-consciousness. "Who decorated this for you?"

"I did it myself. Color and fabric are my forte." She lowered her lashes demurely. "I am a clothing designer by trade, you may remember."

For some reason she felt more secure in an innocuous taunting relationship with him than with the man-woman one he had implicitly introduced upon arrival. Usually very confident of her abilities, she wasn't sure she could handle this male animal, she admitted privately. He had a knack for keeping her off balance.

"I wouldn't have thought you would go in for the natural look." He perused the room more carefully. "I like it," he finished softly.

A smile flickered briefly over her expressive lips, and he realized it was characteristic of her. Her smiles came and went quickly. In actuality she was a reserved person. Also determined and willful, he reminded himself.

But her lips were fascinating. They moved quickly and precisely as she spoke. When she wasn't speaking, or when that flash of a smile wasn't present, they rested neatly against each other, their outline clear and well-defined. She had no dimples, but there was a tiny mole near the left corner of her mouth. He wanted to kiss it.

Astonished at the strong impulse, he frowned heavily and saw the animation leave her face, to be replaced by a calm expression and a defiant glance. Ah, Kim as he knew her. The tough businesswoman. He relaxed. "Now about Australia," he began.

Getting directly to the point, she said, "I really can't spare the time to come to your aunt's boutique opening. I have a grand opening myself this next week. Then I'm off to Paris for the shows. There just isn't a spare moment."

Sean walked over to the dry sink and poured a glass of red wine for himself. He glanced at Kim, who shook her head. He returned to the sofa.

She noticed that he made himself right at home, and she resented it. Why hadn't she offered him something? Layna came in with a tray of chips and dip. "Hello," she said when she saw Sean. Her keen gaze ran over his handsome physique, then settled on Kim. Kim could almost see the wheels turning in her friend's head.

"Layna, this is Sean Stevenson, a . . . friend from out of town. Layna lives across the street and saves my parties from disaster by preparing the food," Kim said, introducing the two.

She watched them size each other up, then they smiled as if an understanding had been established. She was imagining things, of course. Really, it was a good thing she could relax somewhat now. She was obviously working too hard.

"Kim is a wonderful cook when she puts her mind to it," Layna defended her friend. "Which is about once a year," she added with a laugh.

Sean's deep laughter joined in. He was extraordinarily attractive, Kim admitted. He was being charming tonight, just as he'd said he would. Because he wanted something from her, she reminded herself.

"That looks delicious. May I try it?" he requested, pointing to the salmon-and-cheese dip.

While he sampled the food and talked to Layna, Kim tried to regain her composure. She didn't seem to be able to find a neutral ground tonight with Sean. When he had made those sexy remarks, it had changed something between them that had been maintained in a fine balance for more than two years.

Fortunately the doorbell announced the arrival of other guests, and she had an excuse to move away from that redheaded giant, who suddenly unnerved her as few people ever had.

"Hi, come on in," she said to the artist who lived upstairs. He tossed her a bouquet of yellow and red carnations, gave her a smack on the cheek and called a greeting to Layna while strolling toward Sean with a hand outstretched. The men shook hands while she introduced them. "Cecil...Sean. He's from out of town."

"Mostly France, sometimes Australia." Sean filled in the facts on himself when the artist questioned him. After talking briefly with Cecil, he ambled over to the door and stood beside Kim when the next guests arrived. She found herself introducing him as if he were her special guest and was annoyed by it.

The light in his eyes suggested he knew exactly the reaction he caused in her. What he didn't know, she thought in amusement and with slight exasperation, was that she felt quite proud, too. Sean Stevenson was one of those people who would be at home anyplace in the world, in any stratum of society. She was sure he would talk to a village artisan with the same air of respect and friendship he would show a world-renowned business leader.

"Darling, hello!" Lillie Kissenger rushed in as if she had only a moment before dashing off to an important engagement. She was wearing an outfit that Kim had designed for an "at-home" evening with a very special person. The black satin pants had an insert of beige lace at each side seam, going up to the knee, and the same lace lined the top of the spaghetti-strapped bodice, showing off the creamy globes of her generous breasts. It wasn't what Kim would have chosen to wear to a cocktail party.

"I can't stay," Lillie explained, breathless in her hurry. "I've got to go to a party sponsored by the British ambassador to welcome his replacement. Who's this?" She gazed up at Sean with big blue eyes perfectly made up in a flawless face.

Kim found herself hesitant to make the introduction. She stood quietly while Lillie gushed over "the most gorgeous man I've met in ages, simply ages," and Sean said something complimentary back to her. They talked for a few minutes.

"Darling, can you give me a hint, just a hint, about your new collection? You know I won't be present Wednesday," Lillie said to Kim. She wrote an "about town" column for the morning paper. At one time she had been the fashion reporter.

"Think tulips," Kim said, obliging her. She had based her spring collection on the shapes of tulips at the flower show she had attended in Holland several months ago. Bell-shaped skirts and waist-length jackets and frilly blouses in bold primary colors dominated the theme.

"That sounds divine." Lillie swung back to Sean, ignoring her hostess in favor of the most handsome male in the room. Kim greeted her next guest.

Later in the evening, after everyone had arrived, she asked Sean to keep an eye on the punch supply at the bar while she went into the kitchen to see if Layna needed any help. In truth, she needed some distance from him in order to regain her poise.

Lillie's unrestrained flirting had made her feel, well, sort of disgusted, although she didn't recall it ever bothering her before. The reporter had covered her first design show several years ago and written an enthusiastic article about it.

When Kim returned to the living room, it was to see Lillie leaning confidentially against Sean as she chattered away at him. His eyes met Kim's over the other woman's head, and he smiled. Kim relaxed. Lillie wasn't the type to attract him. He didn't like career women. He probably thought the "little woman" should stay at home all the time, keeping supper hot and the house tidy until her lord and master deigned to return and honor her with his company. She thrust her chin into the air defiantly and glared at him. He narrowed his eyes in playful menace, grinned, then looked down at Lillie. He was playing games, enjoying himself.

Later, after Lillie went on her way, Kim heard him discussing the federal budget with a sociologist from the city university.

"How come you know so much about our budget?" Kim asked in a spare moment when she and Sean met at the trestle table.

"I read." He gave her a wink, loaded a small plate to overflowing and went off to resume the discussion.

She caught a reflection of herself, smiling and watching him walk away, and realized that she was having a good time. Glancing at the thirty or so people drifting around the living and dining rooms, she thought everyone else was, too.

It was after eleven before the last guests left. Layna had gone home long ago. Restless, Kim cleaned up the kitchen and straightened the living room before going to bed. She hated to get up and face a messy house.

After getting ready for bed, she turned out the lights and stood by the window. A storm had come up, and rain was falling, not heavily but steadily. A wintry storm, cold and dreary, even though fall had barely begun, she mused.

In Australia it would be early spring. Would the small crocuses be pushing up through the snow? she wondered. Did it ever snow in Australia? She didn't know. In fact, she had never thought about it before. She would ask Sean the next time she saw him.

With a guilty start she realized she hadn't noticed when he left. Well, he had apparently accepted her word that she couldn't go to his aunt's store. Funny, she hadn't thought he would give up so easily.

Maybe he was planning to see her at the salon tomorrow. She wouldn't be there. She was taking the day off to spend with a friend in the country. The manager could handle any details or problems that came up. She had had all the hassle she could take for a while.

Climbing into bed, she thought of Sean's broad chest. It had been like warm granite under her hands when she had run into him. His hands had been gentle when he had steadied her, but she had known that they would be. She also knew he was tremendously strong, for she had seen him help Martin move some furniture once, and had seen him swimming in the Holdens' pool. A woman could feel safe with a man like that. He would protect her and cherish her and love her all his life.

For an insane moment Kim let herself dwell on the vision of her as that woman. What would it feel like to be Sean's woman? With a restless ache inside she acknowledged she would never know.

"He's some man," Layna had confided before she went home.

Yes, some man . . . but not the man for her.

2

KIM WOKE at her usual early hour. She smoothed the sheets, pulled the comforter over the bed and tucked her gown under her pillow before splashing water over her face and pulling a comb through her tousled curls. Slipping into a robe of golden silk that made her feel as if she was walking in sunshine, she headed for the kitchen to put on a pot of coffee.

After the coffee maker was going, she strolled through the living room, yawning and stretching as she went, and retrieved the Saturday-morning paper from the stoop. Heading back across the sand-colored carpet, her scuffs slapping with friendly beats against her heels, she heard a noise in the study.

She froze.

Her heart went into overtime, and her thoughts raced in a mad circle through her brain. Setting the paper on the sofa, she slipped out of her house shoes and silently picked up the poker from its brass stand beside the fireplace.

Hardly daring to breathe, she approached the closed door cautiously. With cold fingers she turned the knob, not allowing herself to think about what was on the other side. She saw nothing as she peeked around the edge.

Stepping inside, she scanned the room. It was a picture of serenity with the early-morning sun slanting through the miniblinds and falling in bars of light on the easy chair. And yet she had the disturbing sensation that indicated another's presence.

A whisper of sound stirred the air, and the hair stood up on the back of her neck. One step at a time, on tiptoe, she crept over to the sofa and looked over the high back.

"Oh, for heaven's sake," she exclaimed.

Sean rose to a sitting position and stared at her in perplexity for a moment, then he looked all around the room as if wondering how he got there. Then he grinned.

"Good morning," he said cheerfully. "Do you always creep up on your guests like some crazy woman and bash them on the head?"

Kim lowered the poker. "What are you doing here?" she demanded, her fear turning instantly to anger.

He covered a wide yawn and pushed the afghan off his shoulders. His jacket and vest lay over the sofa arm, and his shirt was open halfway down his chest, disclosing a thick, curling patch of dark hair that gleamed with coppery highlights when he shifted and a bar of sunshine hit it.

She stared, fascinated in spite of her indignation.

His eyes widened slightly as she walked around the sofa and stood between him and the window. "You'd better move," he said, his voice suddenly sounding very deep and husky.

Glancing down, she saw that the sun had transformed her robe into a shimmering, rippling waterfall of liquid gold. Her figure was also clearly defined as a silhouette within the golden aura of light. She moved back toward the door, aware that his eyes never left her.

"You didn't answer my question," she reminded him dryly, recovering her poise. "What are you doing here? How did you get in?" Another thought occurred to her. "Did you . . . did you sleep here all night?"

"I'm afraid so," he confessed.

"Why?"

He observed the tightening of her mouth as her anger returned. "I've slept about four hours in the last two days. I got bored with the party, and I still needed to talk to you, so I came in here to wait. The next thing I knew you were threatening me with the poker." He glanced at the weapon still clutched in her hand.

"I see," she said slowly, not at all sure that she should accept this simplistic explanation. It sounded too pat. She took a deep breath and her breasts rose enticingly against the golden silk. "Well, you can go now."

He stood and stretched, then leisurely fastened his shirt except for the top two buttons. "I didn't realize the sight of a man's naked chest bothered you," he murmured.

She lifted one brow. "Hardly. But it does bother me to have an uninvited overnight guest." She whirled and walked out.

After replacing the poker in its stand and her scuffs on her feet, she went into the kitchen and poured a cup of coffee for herself. After a second's thought she sighed and went to the door. "Do you want some breakfast?" she yelled.

"Yes," he called.

Opening the refrigerator, she took out eggs and butter and the bread she kept in there because otherwise it molded before she could finish off the loaf. She heard her shower come on.

"Oh, please do make yourself at home," she muttered.

Just as she placed the plates of scrambled eggs and toast on the table, he walked in, fresh and clean shaven, wearing his dark trousers and his dress shirt unbuttoned halfway down his broad chest, his socks but no shoes, and took the seat she indicated.

"Did you find everything you needed—my razor and shampoo and toothpaste—"

"Yes, and your hairbrush and talcum powder," he added amiably. His eyes were laughing at her.

"I can see you aren't going to feel the least qualm," she said, pouring two glasses of orange juice and handing one of them to her uninvited guest.

Sean lifted the glass in a toast to her. "No," he agreed.

Sighing audibly, she brought two mugs of coffee to the table and plunked them down. Taking her place, she picked up her fork and began eating. He did the same.

"Do you always wake up grouchy?" he asked after a few moments of silent chewing.

"No, only when I think I have prowlers, rapists or murderers in my study," she told him. Her quick smile appeared and disappeared. She felt uncomfortable when he continued to stare at her mouth. She wiped her lips with a napkin. "Do I have egg on my face?" she finally asked.

He shook his head slightly.

Anger bridled within her again. Then she saw his eyes. Pure, rampant male hunger showed in them. She swallowed, suddenly nervous around him.

Wait a minute, she reprimanded her runaway emotions. This was Sean. She had known him for… "How long have I known you?" she asked. Her voice came out huskier than she would have liked.

He blinked and looked away. "Years."

"Yes, but how many?" she probed.

"Two, almost three."

She was quiet as she thought about it. That didn't seem so long, yet it was a lifetime. "The first time we met was when I came to visit Mary. . . ." She paused, remembering.

"You came because of Martin," he reminded her with the harsh honesty she had come to expect from him regarding her.

The smile flashed on her mouth and lingered. "Yes, Martin. I knew him as a child and loved him for years. I wanted to see what Mary was like, what kind of woman he went for."

He shrugged and helped himself to strawberry preserves, which he spread thickly on a piece of toast and proceeded to devour along with the heaping mound of eggs. Not sure how many he could eat, she had scrambled three for him and one for her. She saw she hadn't been wrong in her estimate of his capacity.

"You haven't recovered from your puppy love for Mary, have you?" she accused, amused by a sudden insight. "You still moon over her as if she were some kind of Greek goddess mingling with us mortals."

That much she had realized about him on that first visit to their friends' country house in upstate New York. He had thought the sun rose and set on Mary. His attitude had hurt her feelings a little. Mary was a wonderful person and so was Layna. There were different ways of being wonderful. Not everyone had to be the same, or else the world would be a dull place.

Sean gave her a piercing glance, and for a second Kim was afraid she had gone too far, a trait that was all too common with her, she had to admit. But instead of anger, she saw that he found her accusation merely humorous.

"Mary is a very desirable woman and a loving one. And yes, I care for her. She's also my friend's wife. I would never do anything to hurt or betray the trust of either of them."

Kim was ashamed of her below-the-belt barb. "I'm sorry. I shouldn't have said that."

He laid his fork on the plate and picked up the juice, drinking the entire contents before replacing the glass on the table. He studied his hostess for several long seconds before he spoke again.

"No, I'm the one who should apologize. I sometimes find myself deliberately saying things to provoke you. For some reason you make me feel defensive. I'm just not sure what I need to defend against—your aggressive, opinionated ways . . . or my clamoring libido."

She choked on her toast.

He chuckled at her wide-eyed stare. "Well, you are damned attractive, and it is damnably intimate to be sitting across the breakfast table from a beautiful woman dressed in a silk robe. You aren't wearing anything under it, are you?" His gaze ran over her upper torso with lazy interest.

Her nipples immediately came to attention, thrusting against the silk. For the first time that she could remember, ever, Kim blushed.

"Hmm, interesting," he observed, taking in her emotional as well as physical reaction.

Her laughter rang out, a silvery sound of genuine mirth, and he was intrigued.

"So are you." Her eyes tossed a challenge at him. "I've never quite known where I stood with you. You always seemed to disapprove of me."

"And you seemed to consider me a threat to your feminist views," he retorted equably.

He stood, gathered the plates and carried them over to the sink. She took the glasses over, and while he rinsed the dishes and put them in the dishwasher, she wiped the table with a paper towel and poured them fresh coffee. He finished with his chore and started to the table just as she turned from putting the pot back on the coffee maker.

His hands reached out and caught her around the waist, steadying her as she nearly careered into him. They stood there, shafts of sunlight falling over them.

"Like holding a sunbeam in my hands," he murmured, his grip tightening when she stirred restlessly. His thumbs traced endless circles on the silk.

They gazed at each other silently. Kim felt that some momentous event was at hand, that she was about to make an important discovery....

Her breathing became intermittent as his hands slowly glided up her sides and paused beneath her breasts. Steadily, inexorably, his thumbs moved upward. They coasted across her sensitive nipples.

"Don't," she whispered.

"Why?" he questioned. "I've wanted to do this since I saw you yesterday, maybe before that. Maybe since I've known you."

There was wonder in his voice, a question in his eyes. He seemed hesitant, and at the same time caught up in an emotion that he couldn't or wouldn't, fight. "Perhaps that's why I was always on guard around you," he continued.

"Because you wanted to . . ." She wasn't sure what he wanted to do.

"Kiss you?" he suggested. "Make love to you?"

"Is that what you want?" she asked, trying for a light tone and failing. She wanted it, too, desperately, longingly. What was the matter with her? She was a mature woman, she could control her biological urges.

But this was more than biology, some part of her insisted. It was magic, morning magic as wild and tempestuous as any midnight tryst could be. Kim Troussard and Sean Stevenson—who would have thought it? she wondered hazily as his lips descended onto hers.

His kiss was like him—warm and firm with gentleness overlying an inner hardness that was appealing and exciting.

One large hand cupped one of her breasts while the other slid down her back and onto her hips, pressing her to him and leaving no doubt that what he said was true: he did want her.

Seductively he brushed back and forth against her thighs, never letting the contact between them decrease. His fingers dug into her flesh hungrily but carefully.

Her breast swelled to fit his hand, and she grew warm and weak with the force of desire he awoke in her. Her arms instinctively sought the strength of his shoulders, and she drew him closer to her.

"Kim," he said against her mouth, his lips nipping at hers, passion and laughter mingled in the word. "I'm drowning," he whispered. "Are you?"

"Yes," she responded, no thought of lying entering her mind. She wanted him with a tempestuous yearning that seemed new and different from anything she had ever experienced; yet, for her, there had to be more. Reluctantly she pulled away from him.

He tried to coax her back, his mouth moving over hers, twisting, taunting, tempting. When she turned her head, he moved down her neck to her throat, to the breast he exposed to his hungry eyes as he tugged lightly on the robe.

"Beautiful," he said.

He was lost in passion, in his desire for her, she realized and was proud. But . . . "This isn't enough," she told him, wedging her hands between them and pushing at his chest.

"You're right." He swept her into his arms and started for the bedroom.

"No, not that, either."

He stopped, holding her high against him. He was so disappointed at the refusal in her face that she almost relented until better sense prevailed. "No?"

"No," she said firmly. She moved and he let her slide out of his arms. Smiling to soften her decision, she spoke. "I prefer being friends to being lovers."

"Can't we be both?"

"Probably not."

She was crisply sure. In control once more, she walked a few steps away from his alluring warmth. Layna had been right. He was some man. He knew just how to hold a woman, how to kiss her and stroke her. Her flesh tingled at the thought.

He rubbed his chin thoughtfully. "You know, I think that's what always irritated me about you. You decide and that's that. You never change your mind or give another person the chance to present his case."

"I think you presented your case rather well." She frowned slightly and opened her hands to indicate the two of them. "I don't know where this passion between us came from. I don't understand what caused it to erupt—" she stopped and looked at him, remembering their words from yesterday "—but I am sure it isn't wise to encourage it. What do you want from me?"

He visibly relaxed. "Do I need to spell it out?"

Her sharp glance didn't quell his sardonic humor. "You want some fun in New York, but I don't have time to give it to you. I have a great deal of work to do and a short time to do it in."

Sean folded his long frame onto the living room sofa and picked up the paper that she hadn't gotten around to reading. "You're very conscious of time."

"It has a way of getting away from you," she snapped, angry at his cavalier dismissal of her very real concern. An involvement between them would be foolish. What would be the point? Where would it end? "If we made love...to you it would be a one-night stand."

He cocked his head to one side, his eyes narrowing to turquoise ribbons as he studied her. "What would it be to you?"

"A commitment," she answered promptly. She watched his expression. "That surprises you, doesn't it? If you knew me, you'd know that I don't take life lightly."

But where was the humor she was usually able to summon when feelings came too close to the surface?

What, in the space of a few hours, had Sean Stevenson done to her?

She was overreacting, she told her flayed emotions. Both of them were tired and had yielded to the inexplicable chemistry between them. That was all this was.

He pushed himself up and came to her with a swiftness of motion that would have sent a timid person scurrying for cover. His hands on her shoulders gave her a little shake.

"Maybe I don't, either," he snapped, annoyed with her implied criticism. "Nothing happened! Nothing is going to happen! And I'm sorry for what *did* happen!" he finished in exasperation. "How do you women manage to twist things so that men are always in the wrong?" He gave her a final shake, and she glared balefully at him, a sparrow defying an eagle. A long silence ensued while each tried to outstare the other.

Sean's mouth twitched, Kim's lips trembled suspiciously. They burst into laughter. Collapsing on the sofa, they rocked back and forth, clinging to each other. The whole morning had been totally incomprehensible.

When they finally regained control, he pushed her upright and patted her rear. "Since you value your virtue so highly, you'd better get something more substantial on it than that silk wrap, sweetheart."

It was the first time he had ever used a casual endearment with her, and they realized it simultaneously.

"Right, darling," she mocked and dashed down the hall toward her bedroom. The doorbell rang. "Get that, will you?"

"Sure."

The sound of a man's voice asking for her brought her to a dead stop. "Ohmigosh," she muttered and whirled about.

"Connelly, I forgot all about our plans," she cried, returning to the living room and holding out a hand in apology. Sean watched them with great interest.

"Perhaps I should have phoned first," Connelly McClendan said apologetically, his glance going from her robe-clad body to Sean's rather casual state of attire. "Did I, uh, get the dates mixed up?"

"No," she said quickly. "No, I...we... That is, Sean is a friend from out of town, and he came by for the party last night—it's too bad you couldn't make it—and...and then—"

"And then I decided to relax in the study while waiting for Kim to get rid of her guests and ended up spending the night," Sean helpfully put in. He smiled broadly at Connelly.

Kim felt heat rush all the way up to her hairline. Sean made it sound as if she had invited him to stay over. She flashed him an angry glance before smiling at Connelly. "That wasn't the way it happened at all," she stated firmly. "He went to sleep on the sofa. I didn't know he was in the house until I heard a noise in there this morning. He scared me witless."

She arched a defiant brow at Sean as she told the truth. Connelly responded with a polite, understanding smile.

"Actually she scared me," Sean butted in. "Waving a poker over her head and threatening to hit me with it, even after she saw who it was." He gave her a mock scowl, but the gleam in his eyes as he looked her over was anything but fierce. "Dangerous woman," he murmured huskily. He gave Connelly a manly wink.

Kim knew drastic action was called for. "Connelly, do come in and have some coffee while I get dressed. Sean was just leaving." She gave him a very telling glare.

He assumed an innocent expression. "We haven't had a chance to talk yet," he protested. He turned to Connelly. "I'm only in town for a short stay. Do you think you could make it another time? This is a family affair involving something Kim is supposed to do for my aunt."

"Well, sure," Connelly agreed at once, like the perfect gentleman he was. "We were only going to look at some land I'm thinking of buying. It would probably be boring, discussing titles and restrictions with the real estate agent, anyway."

"I knew you'd understand," Sean said.

Kim didn't believe anyone could look so pure and be so black-hearted. "Wait a minute," she snapped. "Don't I get a voice in this decision? After all, it's my day off you're deciding. I'd like a ride in the country."

"Kim, this is important," Sean said sternly.

"Perhaps you'd better listen to him," Connelly said worriedly, "if it's a family problem. We can make it next week. I'll call you." He took her hand, gave it a squeeze, smiled warmly and turned to go.

"I can't. I'll be too busy getting ready for the opening, and then I have a tr—"

"These female tycoons are hard to pin down, aren't they?" Sean remarked to Connelly confidentially. "But another time, then, old man, and thanks for your cooperation." He closed the door.

Kim stood there dumbfounded. "You... you lout, look what you've done. Oh, get out of my way." She tried to push him aside, but that was like trying to move the Empire State Building. He didn't budge.

"Honey, you can't go running down the street after a man in your nightie. It wouldn't look right." His grin was full of self-satisfaction.

She stuck her hands on her hips, her eyes flashing with temper that he had dared interfere in her life. "I just met him the other day. He's one of the nicest people I've ever—"

"But not for you, General," Sean countered. "You'd order him around, and nice guy that he is, he'd try to accommodate you, then you'd end up hating him for being a milksop, and he'd never know what he'd done wrong. Much better to break it off now," he declared wisely.

"I wish I could knock you over," Kim raged. She stalked away from him, turned and stalked back.

Sean tried to keep a straight face. She was magnificent in her anger, a lioness with a mane of dark hair flying around her face, her golden robe swirling about her slender body, opening briefly to disclose a shapely leg to the knee, and her eyes spitting fire and brimstone.

"I wish I were strong enough to throw you out on your nose, you redheaded hyena."

He couldn't stand it. When she stopped in front of him, he pulled her against him and kissed her. For twenty seconds she was stiff in his arms, then she answered his passion with wild abandon, searing him with her heat and the sudden explosive tension of her desire. Her body molded to his, and he burned wherever she touched him.

Kim's anger dissolved into a torrent of need that originated from her turbulent emotion of a moment before, but she knew the fury was only a catalyst for more powerful sensations. The earlier experience of being in Sean's encompassing arms and the urgent attraction she felt for him were also part of it.

After a few minutes she realized he wasn't intensifying the embrace but was letting her expend her emotional energy on him. When she was drained, he held her against his chest and stroked her hair for a long time.

"I don't understand," she said, lifting her head. Why wasn't he carrying her to bed as he had started to do before Connelly had shown up? She was filled with an aching need for him to hold her and make love to her.

"Neither do I," he answered, "but I can't take advantage of you right now. You're vulnerable."

"No one's ever said that to me before." His tenderness was as unsettling as his passion. And she didn't understand either one of them.

"Perhaps they should have."

"I was angry with you. You ruined my day. Why did I kiss you?" she whispered, close to crying and unable to think why. It was all so ridiculous.

"Strong emotion can sometimes do that, turn into something entirely different. Perhaps it triggered a release of earlier feelings." He turned her and sent her toward her room. "Go change. I think we need a break."

He felt exhausted suddenly. This morning had been one of the strangest he had ever known. He had been exposed to a passion he hadn't thought he was capable of, then to a great surge of jealousy that made him act in a completely incomprehensible manner to Connelly and then to a return of the desire coupled with a tenderness for her that was entirely foreign to the feelings she usually provoked.

Too bad he wasn't going to be around longer than the weekend. It could prove to be an interesting relationship. She wasn't what he had assumed at all. And he didn't have time to discover just what she was, he thought regretfully.

"Put on jeans," he called in the general direction of her bedroom. "We'll go to Central Park and have a picnic."

Ten minutes later she appeared in the requested jeans, along with a flannel shirt, a suede jacket, sneakers and a perky knitted cap on her head holding down her tangle of curls. She looked about eighteen.

"We'll go by my hotel, and I'll change clothes," he decided, taking her hand and tucking it in the crook of his elbow.

"I can't go to your hotel room unchaperoned. What would people think?"

"That you're one lucky lady to have a lover like me," he declared modestly. He was glad to see her plucky and full of saucy humor once more. He discovered he didn't like the idea of her being hurt.

She clapped a hand to her forehead. "No conceit in your family."

"Too right. I've got it all," he finished the saying for her, thrusting out his chest as he did.

She grabbed her purse and locked the door behind them. They went swinging off down the street and hailed a cab.

"Too right," she mused, sitting on the hard seat as the taxi jounced along the busy boulevard. "I think that's the first time I've heard you use an Australian colloquialism."

The change in him was swift and unsettling. The humor, the teasing, the sexy challenge—all disappeared like flowers in a hailstorm.

"I haven't really lived there in years," he said.

"Why?" She wasn't afraid to tread on sacred ground.

"My father and I didn't see eye to eye. It was easier to leave the country and establish my own life someplace else." His shrug indicated he didn't want to discuss it.

She nodded wisely. "I know what you mean. But, Sean, sometimes fate has a way of catching up with you. If something should happen to your father, you'd always regret not making it up with him. Don't you ever go home at all?"

"My home is in France. I return to Australia when it's necessary. I have several interests there."

His cool tone warned her not to trespass, but tenacity was one of her traits. "I meant to see your father."

"I see him on family occasions, holidays and all. We're on speaking terms." His glance was stony. "Does that suit you?" he asked mockingly.

"What happened between the two of you?"

"None of your business, General."

Her smile appeared briefly. "I know you think I'm bossy and prone to giving orders, but I wish you wouldn't call me that. It sounds terribly uncomplimentary."

"Then don't meddle in my private affairs." There was a small silence. He heaved a deep breath. "I'm sorry for snapping, but let's drop it, okay?"

"And I'm sorry I said anything about your relationship with your father. You're right. It isn't my concern."

"Look, let's just have fun today. You've obviously been working hard. So have I. Let's take the day off. No cares. No worries. No quarrels between us. Okay?"

She considered pursuing the topic, but the firm set of his chin told her he wouldn't be receptive to anything she said. He obviously thought her meddlesome, but he was stubborn. A grin tickled the corners of her mouth. Stubborn . . . and incredibly handsome.

"Yes," she agreed. "We have only this one day. We'll make it the best ever between us."

She stuck out her hand, and they shook on it. He put an arm around her shoulders, and she was aware of his hand near her breast. Her skin burned all the way through her jacket and shirt. Who would have thought they'd have this much chemistry between them!

3

"FASTER. KEEP UP." Sean pulled Kim along the path at a reckless pace.

"No fair," she protested. "I have to take two steps to your one. I'm jogging, and you're strolling."

She pulled her arm loose from his grasp and dashed ahead in order to plop down on a vacant bench. Taking her jacket off, she fanned her shirt back and forth while she caught her breath.

All over the park people were out enjoying the Indian summer day. They ran, jogged, strolled, stood, sat or lay everywhere she looked. Children shrieked and played running games while mothers gossiped. Old men read newspapers and young ones eyed the women in their clingy sports outfits, which seemed to be de rigueur for all ages and sexes.

The leaves had changed hue, but the grass was still green. The earth was a profusion of tints spread by the lavish hand of a color-loving Nature.

"On days like this," she told Sean, "I fall in love with life. Look at the colors of the leaves—brown, russet, crimson, red, red-orange, deep yellow, pale gold. Doesn't it make you want to create something grand?"

Her hands moved in wide sweeps to indicate the scope of the project she had in mind.

"What do you see?" he asked.

"Material," she responded. "Yards and yards of material in fall colors. If only we could capture the texture of leaves, the whispery sound of the wind blowing through them, the delicious crunch they make underfoot." She sighed dreamily.

"Taffeta is sort of crunchy, isn't it?" Sean leaned close so that his breath stirred the air near her ear, tickling her. "And silk whispers delightfully against a woman's skin when her clothing is removed."

"Let's walk." Kim jumped up and ran away like a child too full of spirit to sit for long.

He quickly caught her hand and slowed her down. They ate hot dogs with lots of mustard and relish squishing out the ends and drank colas from cans while standing in the sunshine.

"We need a Frisbee," Sean said. "Let's go buy one." He started to drag her pell-mell after him.

"Wait a minute, Conan the Barbarian. You can save your caveman act for some female who's impressed by things like that," she informed him, digging in her heels. He gave her a mock frown when she forced him to stop. "Besides, I have a better plan."

"All right, what's your idea?" he asked, clearly indulging her whim.

"There's a place near here where we can buy a kite. It's windy today. Whadaya say?" She used her best New Yorker accent—tough, challenging and confident.

"You're on!"

They took off across the park like puppies let loose for the day. Thirty minutes later they were arguing about putting the kite together.

"No, that's the crosspiece. Here's the long one." Kim took one stick out of his hand and put another in its place. She leaned over his shoulder as he slipped the string into the groove cut into the end of the strut, then she gave directions for assembling the crosspiece and adding the plastic tail.

"Does that suit you, General?" he asked, sketching a salute when she took the kite and tied one end of the string to it.

"Not bad for a buck private, but I'll expect you to follow orders more precisely in the future, Soldier," she replied in a gruff voice, living up to his nickname for her.

He rolled his eyes heavenward and asked for patience.

"Come on!" She ran off with the kite, trailing it out on the long roll of string they had bought and watching it over her shoulder as it rose on the breeze. She ignored his indignant shout. When she had the kite climbing on its own, she stopped running and played out the cord until the kite was above the trees. She laughed with delight.

"Give me that!" Sean took the roll away from her and began to coax the kite upward, letting out yard after yard of string.

Kim watched him with a half smile on her face. He had a little nick of a frown between his eyes as he concentrated on making the kite go higher and higher, but he was thoroughly enjoying himself. She was, too, she realized. It had been a long time since she had felt free of worries, and here she had forgotten about the spring show and new store opening entirely.

"I want one of those. I want a kite," a shrill voice shouted near them.

Kim saw a small boy with a bag of chocolate-covered peanuts pointing toward the kite. He tugged insistently at his mother's skirts. The mother leaned down and spoke to him, an obvious refusal, for his face puckered unhappily. He didn't cry but looked resigned to watching Sean play with the toy.

Sean motioned him over. "I'll make you a deal," he said.

"What?" Big brown eyes scrutinized Sean's skill with the kite and grew wistful.

"I'll trade you my kite for two pieces of candy."

The boy looked at his mother to see what she thought of the suggestion. She didn't object. "Okay."

Solemnly he counted out two pieces of candy and handed them to Sean, who popped one into Kim's mouth and the other into his own. He turned over the kite to the new owner.

"Thanks!" the boy shouted after them as Sean grabbed Kim's hand and raced off with her. They ran until they were out of breath, then they flopped on a grassy clearing in the sun and lay there panting. Finally Sean raised himself on one elbow and looked at Kim. She opened her eyes.

"That was nice of you to give the kite to the boy," she said, liking him suddenly for that.

"I can be kind sometimes." He made it sound as if she had accused him of cruelty.

"Yes, I know." Impulsively she touched his cheek, feeling the smoothness of his skin and the underlying hardness of his bones.

He had always been kind to Mary's little boy, Sammy, and to the other children who visited the Holden home. Sean had shown a patience with them that had been surprising...maybe not surprising, now that she thought about it. He had a way with people, young and old.

Except for her, she admitted. So what was it about him and about her that called up this strange wild passion between them? Both of them felt it. It wasn't her imagination. She could see it this very minute in his eyes.

His hair ruffled in the wind, blowing attractively about his broad forehead. The sun turned it to a fiery golden auburn. His rugged features had a clean-cut appearance that spoke of health and well-being, a man in his prime.

"Your eyes are blue with light brown flecks all around the iris," he commented, watching her. He touched her chin to bring her face more fully to his gaze. She wanted him to kiss her. His gaze intensified as if he could read her thoughts. She spoke quickly before he could act upon the inclination.

"Yes. My mom said they started to turn brown but changed their mind. She said that was the first indication that she shouldn't expect to know what I would do next. I was always off trying something new, then changing to something else."

"Where is your mother these days?" He pulled a blade of grass and tickled her under her nose. She pushed his hand away.

"On a world cruise. Several of her friends talked her into going on a Caribbean tour last year, and they had so much fun they decided to do the world on one of those six-month marathons."

"Sounds like fun" was his noncommittal comment.

"I'm really proud of her. For most of my life I thought of her as basically an adjunct to my father. He was much older than she was and rather arbitrary—at least I always thought so. Breakfast had to be at seven in the morning, dinner at seven in the evening, bedtime was nine for me, eleven for them."

"That sounds reasonable." He kept a serious face while she gave him a ferocious scowl.

"Anyway, Mom has now blossomed into a sophisticated woman of the world. She shed most of her charity committee chairman functions and is on an odyssey of personal growth and discovery."

"Ah, yes, you would approve of that." He pulled her to her feet and steered them along the path.

"Yes. She encouraged me to follow my dreams, even though my father was dubious at first."

Sean made no further remarks but walked alongside the lake, apparently deep in thought. She wondered if he was thinking of his problems with his father.

"Did your mother encourage you?" she finally asked, giving him an opening to talk about it, if he wanted to.

He gave her a hard glance from beneath his brows. "Don't push."

Kim shrugged. "Sometimes it helps to share experiences with someone," she suggested, her smile sympathetic.

"I don't need any help."

His tone definitely posted No Trespassing signs around the subject, warning her not to encroach. He was willing to share the day with her—perhaps her bed—but nothing else. She had enough worries of her own, anyway, without taking on his. She had the new line and the new store to think about. The Fifth Avenue store was her special dream, and she wanted it to perform outstandingly well.

She laughed lightly, drawing his aqua eyes to her. "I think all my maternal instincts are focused on this latest project. I'm so nervous about it, and I don't know why. My name is established, my other stores are doing well, so there's no need to be uptight. But I am."

"Perhaps you'd do better to focus your maternal instincts where they belong," he suggested in a repressive manner.

Kim felt a stiffening in every muscle of her body. "They belong where I decide they do."

"Ah, yes," he murmured.

"I hate people who say 'ah,'" she declared. "It's supercilious and phony."

"Thanks. Glad to know I stand so high in your regard," he said, all the earlier warmth gone.

Kim swallowed the biting words that spilled onto her tongue. Here they were, sniping at each other again. "It seems that we've had about as much of each other as we can stand," she said. "I think I'd like to go home."

"Let's go to Staten Island."

"No, thank you."

"Have you ever been there?"

She refused to answer.

"Aha!" He smirked. "Just like most natives, you've never been to see your own landmarks."

"I'm not a tourist. I don't like touristy things." She tried to tug her hand free from his grasp.

But he wouldn't let her get away. He had decided they were going on a sight-seeing trip and go they did. When they got to the pier, he purchased tickets for the Manhattan tour that circled the big island as well as the small one with the Statue of Liberty.

"The water seems choppy," she said thirty minutes later when they were under way. She already felt queasy. The boat wasn't crowded, and they stood by the railing watching the skyscrapers drift past. She put her jacket on and buttoned it up. The wind was cooler on the water.

Sean stood with his legs planted firmly on the deck, his body moving easily with the roll of the boat. He could have been a sailor returning home from foreign ports, he looked so relaxed standing there with the salt spray and wind in his face.

In a few minutes Kim was positive that she should have gone back to her apartment. The boat pitched up and down through the rough waters off Manhattan. The famous skyline leaped around on the horizon. She clutched her stomach.

"I used to sail a lot when I was a kid," Sean yelled over the noise of the engine and the wind.

She smiled weakly and nodded, afraid to open her mouth. How long was this cruise supposed to last? About two hours? She closed her eyes and breathed deeply.

"Look at that beauty, an oceangoing yacht."

Kim opened her eyes to see what he was so enthusiastic about. A sleek ship was slicing through the water near them, frothing through the waves with the grace of a porpoise. The yacht went up and down, the ferry went up and down, her stomach went up and down.

"Ohhhh," Kim groaned and clutched the railing with both hands. She managed to hold back her nausea for a few more minutes but finally gave up the effort as hopeless. Leaning her head over as far as she could, she lost all her recent meals plus several she couldn't remember, she thought dismally. She had never felt so miserable in her life.

One big hand flattened itself on her tummy while the other held her forehead. She heaved and gagged until she was weak. Finally she regained a tenuous control over her stomach.

"Why didn't you tell me you got seasick?" he wanted to know.

"Why didn't you let me go home?" she wailed. She grabbed for the side again.

Sean held her head until the spasm passed, then he helped her to a seat. He went in and dampened his handkerchief and brought it back to her. He wiped her face with surprising tenderness.

"Have you ever been on a boat before?" he asked curiously.

"Never. Except for water-skiing on a lake occasionally," she added truthfully.

"Why didn't you say something?" He was caught halfway between guilt for insisting they take the trip and anger that she had ruined it.

"I did." She opened her eyes to glare at him, saw the water and quickly closed them again.

"Come on." He pulled her to her feet and took her toward the front. "Look only at the far horizon, not at the buildings or the water next to the ship. Buck up. We only have another forty-five minutes on this tub."

It was the worst forty-five minutes Kim could remember as her body alternated between frantic attacks of seasickness and a weakness that left her almost comatose. By the time the boat docked at the pier,

Sean's eyes reflected his deep concern. He took her home in a taxi, holding her clasped to his chest with both arms around her. She couldn't lift her head.

The driver opened doors while Sean carried Kim into the house. Her protests were completely ignored.

"Thanks," Sean said when the cabbie left with a hefty tip in his pocket. He turned his attention back to his patient.

She slumped into the corner of the sofa, looking like a doll whose stuffing had been removed. "You can go, too," she said. "I'll be all right now that the world has stopped playing leapfrog with my insides." She managed a smile at her feeble joke.

"I'd better help you to bed. You're still weak." He took off his jacket and lifted her into his arms again.

"Put me down." The attempt at indignation didn't succeed. "Ohh," she moaned and pressed her face into the groove of his neck. He was warm and smelled of sea and salt and some faint spicy trace of cologne.

In her bedroom he stripped her to her bare skin, found a nightgown of some gossamer stuff and put her into it. "Wow," he said huskily as he directed her into bed. A blaze of desire leaped into his eyes, which he made no effort to conceal.

She climbed between the sheets none too graciously and turned her back to him, wishing she had adamantly refused that stupid boat ride and had returned home ages ago . . . alone!

"Don't worry, I'm not going to attack you," he admonished, his cool tone at odds with the warmth in his gaze. "I don't take unfair advantage of my dates."

"I'm not worried," she muttered. "Can't you recognize the final stages of acute embarrassment when you see it?"

"Ah," he said in comprehension.

"Don't you 'ah' me," she snapped. Groaning, she buried her face in the pillow. When she heard him leave, she relaxed. Finally her poor tortured stomach quieted and she slept.

"HERE, SIT UP."

Kim woke slowly, disoriented. She pushed herself upright and looked around. The night sky was in full-star bloom beyond her window. Sean was standing beside the bed, a tray in his hands. "What time is it?"

"Only about nine o'clock," he said. "I thought you might be getting hungry by now."

He put the tray down and plumped the pillows behind her head as if she was an invalid. Taking two small throw pillows, he placed them on either side of her thighs and put the tray across her so that it rested on them.

"Eat up," he advised, pulling a chair over to the bed and taking a seat. "How does your tummy feel?" He still felt a jot of guilt for insisting on the cruise.

She rubbed a hand over her abdomen. No rumbles or protests from it. "I think I'll live."

His blue-green gaze followed the progress of the spoon from the bowl of soup to her mouth.

"Do you mind? You're making me self-conscious," she complained.

"Sorry." His grin was apologetic. "Do you have a TV?" When she pointed across the room, he got up, opened the cabinet that hid a small set, then tuned in to an old adventure movie. "Is this okay?" he inquired solicitously.

"Yes, fine, I don't care," she mumbled. "Have you eaten?"

"Hmm? Oh, yes, I made a sandwich." His interest was clearly on the melodrama on television.

The very ordinariness of watching TV with him in her bedroom was disconcerting. It lent an intimacy to the atmosphere that she didn't like. It evoked memories of having breakfast with him that morning and the passion that had resulted. It didn't seem like a good idea to be alone with him in her bedroom at night. It made her uneasy.

She glanced down at her nightgown. He had put it on her, had seen her without a stitch on....

"Is the soup good?" he asked, returning to a chair that looked too spindly to hold his weight.

"Yes. Where did you get it?" It tasted homemade, and she knew it couldn't have come from her cupboards.

"Your friend from across the street gave it to me. I told her you had been sick and asked her advice on what to feed you."

Kim gave him an affronted scowl. "Did you have to tell the world that I was seasick?" she demanded, irritated out of all proportion to the deed.

His smile was indulgent. "I didn't tell the world, only one friend," he said patiently. "Finish up. If you eat every bite, I'll let you have dessert." His lashes lowered seductively, promising a much more tempting treat than mere food.

"I don't want any dessert. And I wish you'd go."

She was too vulnerable at that moment. He was acting as if he cared for her, and she knew that was a lie.

For some reason the sparks between them had ignited into a barely controllable blaze—perhaps they were both tired and open to temptation that particular weekend—but that was as far as it went and as far as she wanted it to go. No good could come from an involvement with a handsome entrepreneur who dashed about the world. He probably had women waiting in three countries for him. She wasn't going to be one of them.

"Why?" he asked, lounging back in the chair as if he had nothing better to do than sit with her.

"Don't you have business to attend to?"

"Yes. And I am attending to it," he continued before she could butt in. "I'm wearing down your resistance. I'm killing you with kindness. Soon I'll have you eating out of my hand."

After a second's astonishment Kim burst into giggles. "I'm not going to Australia," she said firmly. "Never."

"Never say never," he advised with a charming tilt to his mouth. His eyes challenged her to defy him.

"Sean, seriously, you're wasting your time."

"I'm going to be in France next week, taking care of some problems at the vineyard. I'll see you in Paris," he stated confidently. "I'll make a special trip to the city."

She thought for a minute and couldn't resist pushing him a little farther. "If I went to Australia—which I'm not—would I see you there, too?"

"You might." His glance was cooler, his emotions guarded.

When he left with the depleted tray, she dashed into the bathroom and brushed her teeth and washed her face. She was brushing her hair when he returned. He took the brush from her and began stroking it through her curls.

Kim felt the heat rush through her at his nearness. His hand ran down her hair as if testing its smoothness, and she felt a trembling begin inside. It was scary to be this susceptible to another person. Not since she was nineteen had she been plunged into confusion merely by a man's touch.

He laid the brush aside and placed both hands on her shoulders. In the mirror she watched his eyes roam moodily over her face and her figure, which was discernible through the fine material of her gown.

"No, Sean," she said huskily.

"No?" His mouth touched the side of her neck and trailed a whisper of kisses over her shoulder. "You're a lovely woman, Kim. I never realized just how lovely."

Slowly Sean turned her to face him, his hands encircling her slender body and rubbing up and down her back, bringing a flush of desire to her skin. He stared down at her for a long time, until she trembled in reaction. Lifting her in his arms, he carried her back to bed.

For a few short, tingling seconds he let her see his longing, but remembering how ill she had been, he tamped the fires down to glowing embers. "You're right," he murmured. "This isn't the time."

He placed her in bed and pulled the covers over her. With the back of one hand he stroked Kim's cheek, noting how young she seemed with her face fresh-scrubbed and free of makeup.

"Rest now," he admonished gently, unable to explain the tenderness he felt for her, especially when she was the most capable woman he had ever met. He returned to his chair, turning his attention to the TV screen where a battle between the good guys and the bad guys was taking place.

When the movie was over, Sean watched the world news. Glancing at Kim, he saw she was asleep. With a grimace he thought of the sofa in the study.

Kim lay curled on her side, one hand under her pillow, a small bundle in the queen-size bed. Her hair spread all around her shoulders, and he reached out without thinking and pushed one strand away from her face. What the hell, he decided.

Turning out the light, he stripped off his jeans and shirt. When he climbed into bed, she moved slightly toward him. Cupping his body around hers, he put his arm over her and wondered how long he would lie awake, thinking of making love to her. He didn't have to ponder long. He fell asleep at once.

THE DOORBELL WOKE Sean up at eight on Sunday morning. Pulling on his pants and raking his hair into some order, he padded barefoot down the hall to answer.

"Hi," Layna said brightly. "Breakfast."

She held out a covered plate. Sean peeked under the napkin. "Homemade cinnamon rolls," he guessed, sniffing appreciatively at the treat.

"Right. How's Kim?"

"Fine, I think. She slept like a baby all night. Come on in, and I'll rouse her."

"I'm awake," Kim said from the hallway. She finished tying her robe around her as she came into the living room.

"How do you feel?" Layna asked.

"Okay. Thanks for the soup last night. I think that was the cure I needed." She smiled at her friend.

"That and about twelve hours' sleep," Sean added. "I'll go put on the coffee." He disappeared into the kitchen with the plate of rolls.

Layna studied Kim with a delighted smile playing around her mouth. "Well," she said significantly.

Kim settled on the sofa in a froth of lace and silk. "What does that mean?"

"I don't think chicken soup was the cure. I think it was that heavenly male who opened the door barefoot and shirtless a moment ago."

Kim went on the defensive. "Nothing happened between us."

"Nothing?"

"He did not sleep with me," Kim stated unequivocally, correctly reading the conclusion in her friend's eyes. "Honest," she insisted when Layna continued to gaze at her.

Layna glanced all around. "I don't see any signs that he slept out here. And he had definitely just gotten out of bed when he opened the door."

Kim frowned. The last thing she remembered was some movie on TV, one of those ridiculous adventures in which lions roamed around in dank jungles instead of on the plains where everyone knew they lived. She had fallen asleep before the end.

Meeting Layna's triumphant gaze, Kim had to smile at the other woman's eagerness to give her a lover. To Layna every male and female must be paired. Living alone was not a natural fact of life to her.

"Really, Layna," Kim protested halfheartedly.

"Don't let him get away," Layna advised.

"I'm not going to catch him," Kim said indignantly. Really, Layna and her matchmaking ways were sometimes too much.

Layna looked skeptical. "Then you're crazy if you don't. He's interested in you. I can tell. Just practice some of that charm I've seen you lavish on your buyers, and he'll fall at your feet like a giant oak."

"*Timm*-ber," Kim called softly.

"He's just the type I see you falling for." Layna became briskly serious. "He would be a strong lover, one who could take your mind off business once in a while." She gave Kim a look dripping with innuendo. "He could take a starving person's mind off a feast."

"Breakfast is ready," Sean said, coming into the room.

Kim and Layna burst into laughter while he assumed a somewhat rueful, somewhat miffed expression.

"Heavens, I've got to go." Layna jumped up and rushed toward the door, obviously determined to leave the new lovers alone. "It's our Sunday to go to the in-laws' house for dinner." She made a dramatic face, waggled her brows at Kim and her fingers at Sean and departed in a rush of cool, damp air. Sean followed and brought in the Sunday paper.

"What was that all about?" he asked, referring to the burst of laughter as he held out a hand to Kim and helped her up. With a hand on her back he guided her to the breakfast table set in a sunny nook of the kitchen. Coffee, milk and rolls were in place. They sat opposite each other.

"Layna thinks we're lovers," Kim answered bluntly. "Or that we should be."

"Ah, that sounds like a promising idea," he murmured wickedly, watching her over the edge of the paper. He took a bite of roll and began reading.

Sighing, she selected a cinnamon bun from the platter in the center of the table and took a section of the paper from the stack. There was just no talking to some people.

"By the way, where *did* you sleep last night?" she remembered to ask later as she loaded their dishes in the dishwasher. "In the study?"

Sean shook his head, and the morning sun seemed to strike sparks from his hair. His grin was unrepentant. "With you." At her indignant start he said, "Well, you didn't need all that big bed to yourself, and the sofa was too short for me. I didn't crowd you, did I?"

"I don't recall you being there," Kim said truthfully. She had slept more deeply than she had in months. She glanced at the clock. "I need to go to the salon today. I want to check that everything got done yesterday." She looked at him with a question in her eyes.

"And I've got a plane to catch at noon." He yawned and stretched magnificently. "First I've got to check out of my hotel. It seems unfair to have to pay for a bed I didn't use." He gave her a teasing glance.

"No one asked you to stay here," she reminded him.

"Your hospitality is overwhelming." He stood and came to her. "Our business isn't finished yet, Kim. I meant it when I said I'd see you in Paris. You'll be there next week, won't you?"

"Yes."

"So it's settled."

"Yes, but not in the way you think." She laughed, sure of herself now that he was going. "I'm not going to Australia," she said in her "and that's that" tone.

He smiled, ambled off to dress and later kissed her goodbye at her door with a passionate, somewhat taunting embrace before releasing her. "The Carillon Hotel," he called back over his shoulder. "Next Saturday night."

"I won't be there, Sean. I mean it," she yelled after him.

He waved and blew her a kiss just before he dived into a taxi. She closed the door against the damp autumn wind and went to her room to dress. She jerked open the closet door and stopped abruptly, her eyes widening in realization.

The Carillon was exactly where she would be!

IT WAS LIKE WAITING for the other shoe to drop. Kim wondered when—and if—Sean would appear. A message left with the concierge said that he would be delayed, but not how long. Saturday had come and gone, as well as Sunday, Monday, Tuesday, Wednesday and Thursday. Friday found her in the grand ballroom of a Parisian hotel with several hundred other fashion-conscious people and the ubiquitous reporters who covered the shows.

She hadn't been impressed with any of the fabric houses' offerings this year, not even her favorite house from Milan, which had held a small, private preview for selected clients the day before. To tell the truth, her mind hadn't been on business the entire week.

Gritting her teeth, her lips a tight line of determination, she vowed to wipe Sean Stevenson from her mind and her dreams. He had haunted her day and night since he had gone merrily on his way with the promise—or threat, if one cared to view it that way—of seeing her in Paris on Saturday.

Not that she was the least bit interested in seeing him again. No, that was a lie. She hadn't forgotten one word of their previous meeting. Or one kiss. Or one touch of his hands. Her body remembered and burned with sensations that she didn't want to acknowledge.

To heck with Sean Stevenson! Who needed that handsome hunk to interfere in her life? Not Kimberly Barrett Troussard, girl wonder and entrepreneur, thirty-one and a smashing success. She nodded decisively.

"Kim! Wait up!" a male voice called to her through the babel of the crowd.

She noted the fashion show was over and that she was following the mob to the reception immediately thereafter. The reporters had already rushed out to file their stories. She couldn't recollect the last few models she'd seen.

"Hi, Dan," she called to a friend from the States. He was a buyer for one of the expensive chains whose headquarters was in California. He had placed a gratifyingly large order for her spring line of day dresses and evening wear the week before.

"Here to size up the competition?" he asked, catching up with her. His dark hair and light blue eyes were a handsome combination. They had lunch or dinner together when he came to New York. She wondered why he didn't interest her as a man. He was good-looking, they had common interests and enjoyed each other's company, but something was missing. They were friends, but nothing more.

"Actually, to look at fabrics," she explained. "Naturally I couldn't resist a major show while I was in town."

"Have you plans for the evening?"

She shook her head.

"How about dinner? I'll pick you up at eight. Are you at the Carillon?"

"Yes. Eight will be fine."

They talked for a few more minutes before splitting up. She wondered if her life was becoming totally predictable when mere acquaintances knew her habits and preferences. Even Sean had known where she stayed.

"Why so serious?" an amused baritone voice spoke behind her.

Kim turned and gazed into eyes the color of tropical waters. Sean. A thrill of excitement competed with a flash of irritation at his unannounced arrival. She tried, without success, to adopt her old attitude toward him. "I think I'm becoming old-maidish," she replied, opting for a wry humor instead.

He looked her over. Her silk dress was scored with a shiny leaf motif over its bronze-toned surface, a blue scarf with bronze leaves circled her head gypsy-fashion, holding her hair in place. Her shoes and purse were blue leather with metallic trim. Vibrant and beautiful, she was a rare example of prime womanhood.

"If that's true, then I must be a doddering old man since I'm thirty-three, two years older than you."

She accepted the roundabout compliment, it being obvious he was far from doddering or old. "Yes, but I'm becoming set in my ways. Everyone knows I stay at the Carillon when I come to Paris. Even you." Her smile flickered over her bronze-pink lips.

Why hadn't he ever noticed how expressive her mouth was? he wondered. All those times they had met at Martin's place and he had never noticed how feminine she actually was. Sexy, yes—he had been fully aware of that—but not of the innate femininity, which was somehow different from sexy. Funny, he had never made a distinction in the traits in other women.

"I saw the name of your hotel written on the desk pad in your study," he confessed. "What time shall I pick you up tonight? Seven? I'd like to get an early start."

"Perhaps I'm not quite over the hill, not with two men vying for my company," she murmured, giving him a provocative glance from beneath her lashes. He was more than conceited if he thought he could appear without a moment's notice and whisk her away on a date.

His brows met over darkening eyes. "Two men?" he questioned softly, dangerously.

Kim watched the gathering of the storm. "I already have plans for tonight," she said sweetly. "Too bad you didn't call before making the trip. What have you been doing all week?"

"Ah, that's the problem. You're mad because I didn't come last Saturday. The problems with the vineyard were more serious than I thought. Some of the men were threatening to strike. I had to iron out that situation first."

"The pickers?" she asked, interested in spite of herself.

"No, most of the crop is in, except for one field of late grapes. This involved a dispute among the permanent help. Two of the old-timers think they're the boss. They had the younger men aligned into camps, and each had declared war. It took some diplomatic effort to solve the problem."

He finished his explanation and looked down at her expectantly, as if all problems were now solved, his and hers as well as the vineyard's.

When she didn't speak, he added seductively, "I thought we'd have dinner at a special place I know."

"The telephone doesn't work between Charente and Paris?" she inquired. She patted him on his hard chest. "You don't have to answer that," she said playfully. "However, I do have a date for dinner tonight. Perhaps the next time you're in town..."

Deliberately she let the suggestion trail off, both of them knowing they wouldn't be in the same town for at least another six months, if not longer.

"I didn't call because I didn't want to listen to your avowals that you had no time to see me," he explained gruffly. "Listen, Kim, I really do need to talk to you. I'll see you after dinner. I'm staying at the same place—"

"I think not. I have no idea what time I'll be in." Her poise was as cool and distant as a model's.

"I'll wait," he announced in a tone that would accept no argument. He turned and strode off.

He walked like a conqueror, she thought, watching his progress through the crowd. He drew the interest of both sexes as he made his way to the door, and several pairs of eyes focused on her when he waved to her before going out. Heavens, he was magnetic in his attractiveness. She accepted a glass of champagne and sipped it to cool her dry throat.

"YOU'RE DISTRACTED tonight," Dan commented, pouring the remaining wine into their glasses. "Is anything wrong?"

"Uh, no, just the usual pressure of business," Kim said, lifting the glass to her lips. She had a slight headache, a result of the champagne that afternoon, she thought. The meal had been delightful, but she hadn't done justice to the medallions of beef in a piquant sauce that tasted of dill.

"Shall we go?" he asked when they'd finished.

"Yes, please."

That evening she wore a black velvet skirt and jacket with a deep ruby blouse that set off her fair skin and dark hair to advantage. A white mink stole whose ends reached her softly rounded hips completed the picture of elegance when they emerged from the restaurant. A taxi was waiting for them.

"A singularly disappointing season," Dan said, continuing the discussion from earlier in the evening after they were on their way. "The market is shifting from Paris to New York."

"I can name a dozen designers who would argue that point with you," Kim said. "But I agree. The popularity of American designers has spread throughout the world."

"Particularly in the casual clothes. Isn't it funny that what used to be casual clothing is now our formal evening wear?" he mused aloud.

Kim murmured agreement. The tailcoat had originally been worn for riding, now it was the height of sartorial splendor.

"Two hundred years from now we'll be wearing jeans and sweatshirts to the theater. What will we be wearing to play in?" he asked.

"Coveralls," she said. "I'm thinking of bringing out a line of them for people who see themselves as trailblazers."

Dan was interested. "If you do, I want to place an order."

Kim was pleased at his eagerness. Her casuals did well in his chain, but his customers would want something more elegant than the rugged wear she had in mind for camping and hiking. Hmm, there was a thought—rugged looks in elegant fabrics for leisure wear. She tucked the idea into the back of her mind.

"Care for a nightcap?" he asked a few minutes later as they entered the lobby of her hotel.

"Not tonight. I think I'll go right up," she decided, her eyes darting around the spacious room. She saw a blaze of hair resting against one of the velvet chair backs and rushed for the elevator. Dan escorted her to her room.

At the door he gave her a quick kiss on the lips. "Think about doing an exclusive for us on the coveralls, won't you? I can guarantee you a special advertising budget."

"I'll think about it," she promised.

"About time," Sean said, walking up before she could go inside and close the door. He smiled at Dan in a friendly fashion. "Just like a woman to keep a man waiting all night," he complained good-naturedly. He ushered Kim inside and closed the door in Dan's rather surprised face.

"Kim, are you all right?" Dan called to her.

"Yes. Sean is a friend," she assured him, bowing to the inevitable confrontation she could see brewing. Might as well get it over with once and for all. She was *not* going to traipse all over the world at Sean's instigation. The sooner he realized that, the sooner their lives could go back to normal.

"Good night, then." Dan sounded puzzled, but he left.

"I told you I didn't want to see you," she snapped at the towering male before her.

Sean glanced at his watch. "It's after eleven. I've been waiting since ten." He was annoyed.

"Tough." She hung her wrap in the closet and yawned loudly to let him know she was tired and in no mood for arguing.

"I can see you need some softening up," he observed, taking a different tack. "I took the liberty of ordering coffee—in case this became a long session."

A knock sounded on the door.

He opened it and let the waiter inside. After the man left, Sean poured them each a cup of coffee and a snifter of cognac. "Here, have some," he invited, playing the gracious host.

"Why don't you just make yourself at home in my suite?" Kim decided an amused, tolerant manner was the best way to handle him. "You are exasperating, you know," she added with just the right touch of asperity.

"Mmm-hmm. You are, too."

She kicked off her shoes and curled up on the sofa, tucking her feet beneath her. His aqua gaze slid over her in a visual caress that left no doubt in her mind that he found her a most desirable woman. It was a heady sensation. One that should be ignored, she reminded herself as her pulse speeded up. She had a mind of her own and was not going to succumb to his masculine charm, potent as it was.

"I like the way you move," he said slowly. "Gracefully, with an economy of motion as if every action is planned before it's performed."

"Thank you," she said, sipping delicately from the brandy glass. He seemed suddenly hesitant. Her own poise took a dip. Did she want him there or not? Different parts of her fought silent battles with other parts; none seemed to win. She was ambivalent about his presence and chagrined about what he did to her reasoning when he was near.

"I've thought about you a lot these past two weeks," he said presently, a reluctant confession.

Kim realized she wasn't the only one haunted by their illogical reactions to each other. Sean was off center over them, too. She dropped the insouciance in favor of her usual forthrightness. "Don't play games with me, Sean. I don't participate." She looked at him levelly over the glass.

"I'm not. You've knocked me for a loop, to tell you the truth. I want to make love to you." He returned her gaze with a candid openness of his own.

His honesty jolted her into the realization they couldn't go back to their former ways of dealing with each other. The old foundation of dislike and amused tolerance was no longer there, and she didn't know what had taken its place. She and Sean had shared too much that weekend in New York. He had seen her ill; she had seen him perform kind deeds. They had laughed together, had played. They had been vulnerable to each other, caught up in a passion neither had understood or wanted. She shook her head at this incomprehensible state of affairs. "No," she said.

"Yes," he contradicted. "But there's no time. Contrary to your opinion of me, I don't indulge in one-night stands any more than you do. I need meaning in my relationships with people."

"All right," she said, accepting his word. "Where does that leave us? We agree not to have an affair due to lack of time and emotional involvement, so what happens now?" Her eyes, dark in the diffused light from the shaded lamp, asked for answers from him.

He smiled, seemingly jovial now that they had gotten past some difficult point in their dealings with each other. "How about a relaxing day together like we had before? Are you busy tomorrow? I promise not to take you on a boat tour of the Seine." He crossed his heart.

Her first inclination was to pointedly refuse, but the challenging way he lifted one brow—he obviously expected the refusal and was marshaling his arguments—caused her to pause. She disliked anyone thinking she was so predictable. With a defiant laugh she agreed and was pleased with his surprised reaction. Her next thought was to wonder at her own actions. Their relationship was as unsettled as her stomach had been on the boat. What was the use in stirring it up further?

"Would you like to see the vineyards?" he invited. "The late grapes are still being picked."

"That's a long trip," she began hesitantly.

"We can leave at eleven, have a picnic lunch on the road, tour the winery, eat an early supper and head back toward Paris around six. How does that sound?"

"Wonderful. I love to sightsee in the country." She held up her glass. "Am I perhaps drinking cognac from Charente?"

"You are." He crossed his legs at the ankles, and she couldn't help but notice the length and the power of them. She remembered how he had looked in bathing trunks, his body cutting through the water at Mary and Martin's with a strength that made that medium his element. "Tomorrow," he said, lifting his glass before bringing it to his lips.

Kim followed him in the toast.

Now that he had her consent for the next day, he didn't press the point of his visit—the Australian trip—but seemed content to talk idly about the week's activities and to listen while she told him of hers. He left at midnight.

It was nice to talk to him without strife or controversy for once, she thought while getting ready for bed. And it was good that they had gotten the problem of their irrepressible attraction to each other sorted out. She liked things clear-cut and in place. Perhaps they could become friends after all.

A RIME OF FROST DUSTED the boulevards of Paris like powdered sugar when Kim looked out the window the next morning. The sky was a crisp blue, the air energetic with cold. She decided to wear a wool pantsuit of nubby tweed. With ankle boots and a knitted cap she would be warm enough if the sun failed to take the chill off.

When Sean arrived at eleven, she was impatiently eager to be off. "Let's go," she demanded, laughing in high spirits. "I feel so good today."

"Why?" He glanced at her out of the corner of his eye before pulling into the fast-moving traffic.

"I don't know and I don't care," she said recklessly. "I'm not going to analyze, I'm just going to enjoy."

The car was warm, and she soon discarded her coat. Her escort whistled in approval when he saw the smoky-blue sweater she wore. "I think I'll just enjoy, too," he murmured, his eyes running over her in sexily familiar ways.

"We agreed that we wouldn't . . . that there wouldn't be anything between us," Kim reminded him.

"But we didn't say anything about looking and admiring." He paused for a long minute. "Or wanting."

"No, we didn't. But we're not to let it get an upper hand," she replied jauntily. In spite of her words, a brief ache sang through her with the piercing sweetness of a fluted melody. Honestly, her emotions were as changeable as a seesaw.

Sean reached over and touched her hand, just one gentle touch that said he understood her feelings. She wondered if he really did. She sure as heck didn't!

"I love the French countryside, the rolling grain fields, the hill country and the mountains." She kept her gaze focused on the view rushing past her window.

"The Riviera?"

She shook her head. "No, that part doesn't appeal to me. The château region reminds me of New York State up where Mary and Martin live. I had such a lovely time there this summer. Little Sammy and I explored the woods and creek for hours. I've often wished I had more time to tour the countryside here."

"Then I'm glad I invited you to come up with me."

They listened to music on the radio. Kim sang along with the songs she knew and relaxed in the warmth of the sun. When they stopped at a sunny meadow beside the road, she found she didn't need her coat.

Sean was the perfect host. He spread a pad on the ground and put a blanket over it. From a woven wicker basket he pulled out servings of boneless chicken breasts, fried light and crispy, a mixed salad of broccoli, carrot slices, beets, cucumbers and radishes tossed with a vinaigrette dressing that made her mouth water and, of course, french bread. He had both wine and coffee.

"Oh, this is perfectly delicious," she exclaimed, licking her fingers after taking a bite of chicken.

"It's nice to feed a woman who appreciates food," he said, wolfing down his own portions.

"Yes, but I have to watch my weight constantly. Do you?"

"Not yet."

"No, of course not," she agreed in disgust. "When you're as big as a mountain, you can eat like a horse."

He threw back his head and roared with laughter at her disgruntled expression. "Mountain, is it? Horse, huh?" he challenged. Sean pushed her down on the blanket and loomed over her. "I think I'll sit on you."

"I didn't mean it! I didn't mean it!" she pleaded shamelessly.

The laughter died in her eyes as she read the change in his. His gaze roamed over her breasts, which were faithfully outlined by the sweater. He dwelt on the quick intake of her breath and its slow exhalation. She tried not to let her chest move as she forced her lungs to a normal rhythm.

"Kim," he said hoarsely.

Longing was written in the darkening of his eyes, and her body answered with a sharp quickening inside. His lips descended slowly, agonizingly, toward hers. When their mouths touched, she felt as if she was shattering into a prism of light. Like a rainbow, she thought.

His chest pressed against her breasts, and he was warmer than the sun. His hair gleamed like fire, and she couldn't resist. Lifting her hands, she ran her fingers into those magic flames that warmed her clear down to her toes.

She responded to the enticement of his lips moving against hers and opened her mouth to him. He at once claimed the treasure, deepening the kiss until they were both breathless and their hearts pounded in unison against their ribs.

His hand stroked along her side, then slid smoothly onto her breast, kneading the burgeoning flesh until her nipple peaked in his palm.

"Umm," she sighed, a demand and a sound of pleasure.

"Your voice is like silver," he murmured, pushing the cowl neck of the sweater out of the way of his marauding lips. He trailed kisses onto her throat. "I knew how it would sound when I made love to you. I've heard it for weeks in my sleep."

Her breast grew heavy and turgid under his skillful caresses. She wanted him to touch her without clothing between them. She wanted to feel his flesh pressing against hers. She wanted his warmth, his strength, his passion.

Her own desires flowered into a hunger that matched his. When his hand left her breast to roam along her hip and thigh, she moaned and tightened her hold around his shoulders.

Finally, with a low groan, he forced himself from her and sat upright, his chest heaving as if he had run for miles, his eyes tightly closed against the passion that raged within.

"God, Kim, I think I could take you right here on the side of the road. I want you that much."

"Yes," she whispered, knowing exactly how he felt. Her attempt at laughter was feeble. "So much for our good intentions." She dared look at him then, her eyes troubled by the feelings they invoked in each other. They had to control this wildness that erupted with a single touch.

Sean opened his eyes and returned her gaze. With one finger he touched her reddened lips. "You're some woman, lady," he said huskily. He stood. "We'd better go."

Quietly they gathered the remains of the picnic and started out once more along the winding road to the vineyard. They were silent for the rest of the journey.

Kim forced herself from her internal musings as Sean turned into the gravel drive to the estate. Massive pillars of fieldstone supported wrought-iron gates that were always open to visitors. The château, made of the same stone, was as impressive as any she had seen in the "château country," yet the informality of the hedges and trees grouped about the grounds made it seem as welcoming as a farmhouse. She knew instinctively that she would love it.

When they got out of the car, they were greeted by the resident dogs, Diet and Gigi, who barked and ran in joyous circles around them before Marietta, the housekeeper, came out to shoo them aside and welcome the two of them.

"Come, come," she invited them inside. "Quiet, you two." She scolded the dogs as if they were wayward children. She didn't appear in the least surprised at the extra guest, and Kim wondered if Sean often brought women here.

The den was a huge room with a fireplace large enough to hold a six-foot log occupying one wall. It had been the original kitchen but now did duty as a family room while a smaller room had been updated to a modern kitchen.

While Sean checked his mail, Marietta showed Kim around the house. The housekeeper was not much older than Kim, but she wore a black dress reaching nearly to her ankles, her hair was drawn into a knot at the back of her neck and her face was free of makeup. She was a village girl who had had the good fortune to marry the overseer of the vineyards, and she took her duties as chatelaine seriously.

When Sean gave a shout, Marietta directed Kim to him, and he escorted her on a tour of the fields, using a pickup truck to drive over the orderly estate. Kim loved the industry displayed by everyone in the wine-growing business. They obviously thought their work was important, and all had an opinion on the quality of the grapes that year. "An average vintage" was the consensus.

They stopped by the winery and sampled some of the first drawings from an earlier corkage. Kim thought it was fine; the vintner and Sean declared it still raw. They tasted the cognac, which was distilled from only the finest white wine, and pronounced it "smooth and elegant." Kim thought it tasted okay, too. She had never been able to tell what made it elegant, as opposed to modest or *ordinaire*.

They returned to the house at four, crunching through the golden leaves of the poplars that lined the stone fence along one side of the drive. It was a glorious fall afternoon, warm enough that they had shed their coats and carried them thrown over their shoulders.

Looking at Sean, Kim decided he epitomized elegance. He was dressed in tan slacks and a black turtleneck sweater with a padded vest over it. His jacket of buff leather was a camel tan and added just the right touch to his expensive but casual outfit. He wore no hat, and his hair picked out rays of the sun and splintered them into shimmering crystals.

He guided her into a library where ancient books rose in row after row of glass-enclosed shelves. She read titles until she came to a group of modern tomes on subjects that ranged from wine growing to economics. There weren't any novels.

"Don't you ever read for fun?" she asked, curious about this glimpse into his mind.

"When I'm flying, I usually try to read something light."

"Kafka?" she suggested as she sank into a deep chair. "Or perhaps one of the Russian authors, the ones who write nothing in less than a thousand pages?"

He laughed at her teasing. "Westerns or science fiction."

She pretended to be amazed. Yawning, she stretched her feet toward the fire. "Isn't it time to start back?" she asked lazily. She didn't want to move.

"Soon. We'll have an early supper first."

As if on cue, Marietta called them into the dining room at that moment. After the meal they returned to the library. He chose a seat beside her, resting his arm on the back of the sofa. She turned to look at him.

"Looks like the fun is over," she commented, seeing the determination in his eyes. She prepared herself for an argument.

"You remember what you said about your mother when I was in New York?" he surprised her by asking.

She nodded cautiously.

"Well, the same thing is happening to my aunt."

"Aunt Mattie?"

"Yes. Her husband died a couple of years ago." He paused and stared into the fire as if seeking the most convincing words. "It was a hard time for her, as if she was lost or something. She seemed to lose her balance in life. We were worried about her for a long time."

Kim could relate to that. A man quite often formed the anchor of a woman's life so that when he was gone, the wife would drift aimlessly. "Everyone needs a sense of purpose," she said, more to herself than Sean.

"Yes," he agreed immediately. "That's why I'm so glad she has finally found something she wants to do. She inherited several department stores, but this boutique was all her own idea, and she has worked extremely hard on it. Like you did on your new store."

He deliberately drew a parallel between his aunt and Kim. She cast him a glance under cover of her lashes, knowing what he was doing but unable to keep from responding to the other woman's efforts. She knew what it was to be determined and yet afraid that that first project was going to fall flat.

"This means so much to her. She needs a success," he went on after a minute of silence. "That's where you come in. You can give her that."

His hand dropped to her shoulder to emphasize the point. Kim warmed under his touch. Needing distance from his persuasive charm, she stood and went to the hearth, standing with her back to the room.

"Under your direction, the project can't fail." Sean went to her. "Please, Kim," he said, almost humbly, as if he knew what thoughts raged through her head.

"That's not fair," she said shakily. How could she resist such an entreaty as this?

"I know, and I wouldn't ask if I didn't think it was important. You're the only person I know in this line of business—"

"Or you would have asked someone else?" Her glance over her shoulder was both amused at and resentful of his tactics.

"No, only you would do. You're the perfect role model for Aunt Mattie—the successful woman, forceful, determined, in control—all the things she needs to develop in herself."

And none of the things he wanted in his woman, she realized. "It sounds as if she's well on her way," Kim said, projecting a brightness she didn't feel.

"This first attempt is crucial. She has to make it, or she might crawl back into her shell . . . and we'll never again see her as she was meant to be."

Kim closed her eyes, wanting to block out the picture he conjured up with his description. She felt as if all women everywhere depended on her answer at that moment.

"You usually take November and December off, don't you?" he inquired softly. "Take a vacation in Australia."

"It isn't that simple. I use that time to work on sketches and new ideas."

"You'd get lots of inspiration there, I'm sure," he predicted. His hands at her waist turned her to face him.

"I know that nothing in our past has warranted it, but would you do this one favor for me?"

She couldn't refuse. That he cared so deeply for his aunt touched her in ways she didn't want to acknowledge. "All right," Kim said, giving in to fate.

Actually, the trip might prove a wise investment if she did gain a new market, she reminded herself, focusing on the practical aspects in order to ignore the emotional ones.

"You will?" he demanded.

"Yes, I'll do it. For one month."

He lifted her off her feet and swung her around and around. She clutched his shoulders and held on.

"Put me down this instant," she ordered. His pleasure in her capitulation stirred anger in herself. She had no reason to want to please this overgrown hunk.

He let her down slowly, her body pressed against his the entire time. When her feet touched the floor, she stayed where she was, with his hands at her waist.

"Now that that's out of the way, you have no reason to think I'm trying to seduce you into anything," he said.

A puzzled frown appeared between her brows.

"Let's stay here tonight," he said. His bright gaze never left hers.

"I have to catch a plane for New York tomorrow." That sounded lame, even to her ears. Why didn't she refuse outright?

"What time?"

She swallowed. "Three o'clock."

"We'd have plenty of time to get back. I could take you to the airport."

Kim gave a little laugh. "The grand farewell?"

His hands tightened at her sides. "Don't be flippant," he snapped. "I don't know what's happened between us, but I do know I don't want it to end like this—inconclusive." His voice dropped to an intimate level. "All my life I'd wonder what I missed because I didn't take you to bed."

His low laughter was like a caress. She tried to think why they shouldn't give in to this madness.

"We . . . we don't even like each other very much."

"Maybe we like each other more than we've ever been willing to admit. There have always been sparks between us. Perhaps we misread the signs."

He waited for her to make the decision, not pressing the sure advantage of an embrace between them. A half smile curved his attractive mouth, and she knew he would accept whatever she said without insisting.

One night, she thought. They could have one night, and having had it, they would probably be over this need to know the other on an intimate level. Yes, it was more than desire: they each had a requirement that could only be fulfilled in the other's arms. It was so strong, this need for each other.

The answer must have been in her expression, for his smile spread over his face and into his eyes. He pulled her to him and buried his face against her neck, kissing her there with hot, moist kisses that burned right down to her insides.

"Kim," he whispered.

It seemed so strange to hear her name spoken in passion by him. What had happened to their logic about brief encounters and meaningless relationships? She didn't know. Closing her eyes, she put her arms around him and responded to the need that raged between them.

"Yes . . . Sean, yes . . . yes . . ."

5

He lifted her in his arms. "I've dreamed of this," he murmured huskily. "I wasn't sure I'd get to live the dream." He climbed the stairs, carrying her easily. His strength excited her.

The masculine force that surrounded him would attract even the most discriminating feminist, she thought. His magnificent body was in perfect tone, his muscles strong but not overdeveloped.

Kim held on to him, exploring him with her hands, soaking his warmth into her skin, feeling as if they were melting into each other, as if they were becoming part of each other.

Wait, she reminded herself. This was just a physical thing, an attraction that had grown like a weed that wouldn't be discouraged, no matter how many times she plucked it from the fertile ground of her imagination. She couldn't seem to tear it out by the roots. Lifting her head from his shoulder, she gazed at his face. His brow was furrowed as if he was concentrating on some terribly important task that couldn't be interrupted.

Sean glanced at her and paused on the top stair. Seeing the troubled expression in her eyes, he waited for an indication of her wishes. "If this is wrong for you, then say so. I don't want regrets between us."

"No regrets," she averred.

He turned down the hall and entered a room at the end. The chamber was large, with a ceiling that soared a good twenty feet above them. The massive four-poster bed stood four feet off the floor and had polished oak steps leading up to it. An armoire and dresser matched the bed in size and elegance.

At the foot of the bed was a long bench. He put her down next to it. Without fumbling or awkwardness he began undressing her. "Lovely," he said, touching the blue lace that edged her breasts and hips before removing the rest of her clothing, then his own. His hands settled at her waist, urging her toward him.

"Ahh," he murmured in satisfaction when he at last brought them together. With just her nipples buried in his thick, dark curling chest hair, he glided his hands upward until he could cup the fullness from below.

He smiled sexily, pleased with her response. "I want you as I've never wanted anyone before, with a fire that burns my insides to cinders every time I think of you." He was serious, not teasing.

"Yes," she said, admitting she felt the same.

"But I'll be careful with you."

"I know. I'm not worried. . . ." Her voice trailed off in wonder at the gentleness of his strength, the intensity of his passion. His regard was one of fierce tenderness. "Let me touch you," she requested.

He released her and stepped back, indicating his willingness to let her set the pace. "I used to notice you in the pool," she murmured, running her hands over his wide shoulders and down his arms. "Flex."

Smiling, he flexed his muscles for her, then relaxed them as she explored his hands, holding them cupped in her palms while she studied the lines across his.

"You will have a long life," she intoned like a fortune-teller. "And great happiness." She smiled up at him and saw him catch his breath.

"Sorry, love, but I'm more impatient than I thought." With a rapid motion, as if he couldn't stand waiting for another second, he lifted her up the three steps and placed her on the bed. He quickly slid in beside her, his large frame partially covering her, his thighs meshing with hers.

He ran his hands over her, her breasts, her abdomen, her hips and thighs. She liked his touch on her. Her own explorations seemed to inflame him. He wasn't a bashful lover, and he let her know when she pleased him with low, throaty murmurings that she found endearing as well as exciting. She wanted to give him as much pleasure as he gave her.

His mouth roamed hungrily all over her face and neck and back to her lips. She opened her mouth and welcomed him. Their tongues met, touched tentatively, then aggressively. He moved further over her, crushing her into the deep, comfortable mattress.

"I love the feel of you against me," she told him.

"You're like silk," he complimented, running his hands all over her. "Smooth. Soft. And sweet, so sweet."

His lips left an imprint of kisses down her throat and on her breasts. Her breath refused to function when his mouth, hot and moist, took her nipple. He circled the tip with his tongue again and again, until the sensation was more than she could bear. She writhed against him.

He laughed softly, then gasped when she retaliated with her own torturous explorations. She followed each clean-cut line of his body until she knew his contours perfectly and all the places he liked to be stroked and kissed.

"Sweet darling," he said, not sparing with his endearments. "You're wonderful, Kim, wonderful."

"So are you." Her voice trembled, and her hands rushed frantically over his back and along the firm flesh of his hips. A slight shudder ran through him.

"Sean." She couldn't find the words to describe all the incredible sensations he produced in her. His hands knew exactly how to touch, where to touch and how long to linger in that one spot before moving on. "Come to me," she invited.

"I wouldn't last a second. Rest for a minute." He smoothed her hair back from her face. "I've always loved your hair. It seems to have a life of its own, drifting around your shoulders like a cape."

His voice was a caress. Husky and deep, it flowed over her like some magic liquid. He smelled clean, of soap and shampoo and some subtle male cologne. All her senses were filled with his essence.

Slowly she ran her hands down his rib cage and onto his hard, flat stomach. Gently she touched him. Smiling at the groan of desire her action wrung from him, she deliberately sought those touches that brought him the most pleasure. He moved seductively under her ministrations.

His mouth took hers as he turned on his back and brought her over on him. His hands stroked from her shoulders to her thighs, and their bodies rocked against each other, moist now with the perspiration engendered by the heat of their passion.

"I'm going to explode if I don't have you soon," he told her, a ripple of laughter in his voice.

She was enchanted. A man who could laugh at himself under these circumstances—under *any* circumstances—was unlike any she had ever known. A sort of tender ache invaded her heart.

For the first time that she could remember, Kim felt cherished. Sean made her feel as if she was some precious gift temporarily given into his keeping. He seemed determined to bring her pleasure, willing to forgo his own until he was sure she was satisfied.

"You are the most wonderful lover," she said solemnly.

"So are you, my love." His lips nibbled at her mouth. "You please me more than I thought possible."

She felt so proud.

He wrapped his arms around her and shifted them to the more traditional lovemaking position. He trailed kisses along her breasts and stomach. She moaned helplessly when he touched her intimately, and when she couldn't take another second, when she was totally lost in joyous rapture, he came to her, pressing into her softness with a sure, steady stroke that melded them into one. She sighed in satisfaction. Their bodies flowed together in a joyous, exultant song of passion, a paean of praise to the ancient ritual of joining—woman to man, man to woman. When the release came, they found it together, an explosion of the senses that bound them in ecstasy for an endless span of time.

Sean held her until her trembling receded, until his own breath moved easier into his lungs. He felt protective toward her, this slender woman who had brought him a greater pleasure than he had ever known.

When he moved to lie beside her, neither of them spoke. He clasped her to him, and she nestled against him contentedly, both of them quiet for a spell.

"Talk to me," he invited lazily when she stirred.

"What about?" She yawned and turned toward him.

"Mary mentioned you had been engaged. When was that?"

"About three years ago." Grinning, she asked, "Why? Was I terribly awkward as a lover?"

He laughed at her lighthearted question, sure that she was fully aware of the devastating effect she had on him. She was generous in the passionate giving of herself. "No, you were wonderful. What happened to the guy?"

He discovered he wanted to understand everything about her. She had always been a mystery to him. He'd thought that after making love to her he would know her completely, but he realized that was an illusion. He had only found that there was more to know than he had suspected.

"He was busy establishing himself, and I was busy establishing myself. Even the greatest love can't last forever without attention."

The simple truth in her explanation touched him. She was one of the most astute people he had ever met, seeing to the heart of a matter immediately and unafraid to act on any problem she ran up against. He pictured her accepting the breakup and carrying on with her life and her work with calm efficiency.

But she had been anything but calm in his arms. A flash of pride burst through him. What they had shared had been primitive and elemental, but graced with tenderness and humor. They had dealt with each other openly and honestly about their wants. For the first time he felt they were friends.

"I'm glad you told me," he said, reaching for her. He touched her tenderly. "I'd like for us to be friends, Kim. Do you think we can?"

She laid her head on his shoulder and her arm across his chest. "Friends," she agreed.

For a while after he went to sleep, she lay awake in his arms. She wondered why Sean had asked her about her engagement, and why she had told him. Not that it was a great secret, but she was usually reserved about her emotions. Making love engendered an intimacy that was hard to confine to one area.

Ah, life was sometimes strange, she thought, then smiled as she realized she had used his favorite "ah" with the sentence. Perhaps the two of them were more alike than it appeared.

She stirred slightly, and his grip tightened as if even in sleep he was determined to keep her. Letting herself totally relax in his embrace, she went to sleep feeling warm, feeling cherished, feeling... The last word didn't come to her.

KIM WOKE TO THE FEEL of kisses being placed with great precision on her cheeks, on her chin and on her forehead.

"Good morning, beautiful," Sean greeted her.

His smile was as bright as the sunshine streaming in the window across the room. His eyes gleamed like turquoise as he looked down at her. With intense concentration he ran his fingers through her hair, smoothing out the tangles that the night and their lovemaking had produced.

"I'd like a bath," Kim said, smiling up at him. "And some breakfast. In that order." She giggled without restraint when he grazed his beard lightly over the groove of her shoulder.

"Ever the practical woman," he admonished, refusing to let her up. He rubbed his nose against hers. When she lifted her lips to his, he teasingly moved away, not letting their mouths meet. He chuckled when she scowled.

"Do you always wake up full of the devil?" she demanded, trying to turn her back on him but without success.

"Always," he said solemnly. "It's a terrible burden, too, always wanting to do this . . . and this . . . and this as soon as I open my eyes in the morning."

She was helpless with laughter by the time he finished biting her in various places. He then went back over the places with kisses that tickled as much as the little sucking love bites had. His hands made their own dashing forays over her.

Finally, when his own breathing was shallow with longing and his control in danger of failing completely, he heeded her demands. Leading the way, he guided her to the bathroom, where he turned on the shower and proceeded to wash her thoroughly.

"I haven't been this clean since I fell in the horse muck when I was five years old and my mother nearly scrubbed my skin off." She gave him a scolding glance.

"I've always had this thing about cleanliness," he murmured, paying careful attention to her breasts.

He stroked her nipples until they contracted into tight buds of desire, then he turned her into the stream of water and rinsed her so that his mouth could take the place of his nimble fingers. His tongue played intimately against her sensitive skin, and her knees became weak. Then Kim returned the favor, lightly soaping him all over and rinsing him.

"Enough," he said hoarsely, dried them off and followed her back to his bed. He found that he liked playing erotic games with her. He loved the way she taunted and teased, the way she became frantic for his touch at a certain point during his lovemaking. She made him feel as if he was the world's greatest lover. With her he thought maybe he was. She seemed to bring out the best in him. "I can't get enough of you," he whispered, a tortured look of longing in his eyes.

She pulled him to her, reveling in the slight abrasiveness of his skin on hers. She loved the lean hardness of his body, the way the muscles bunched and flexed in smooth motions like ropes of steel under her hands.

"I need you," he said with a groan as he nudged her thighs apart so he could lie within her embrace.

He moved deeply within her with steady thrusts that carried them both past the brink of thinking and into the wonderland that only they shared. Together they found the ecstasy and the release, collapsing weakly against each other at the end.

"Can you take my weight?" he asked, fighting for breath. "I don't think I can move."

"Yes, it's okay. Rest on me." She held him for several minutes until her own need to draw breath prompted her to move. He immediately rolled off with a murmured apology.

For another hour they dozed or simply lay in each other's arms, needing no words but only the contact.

Kim was the first to want to play again. She ran her hands over his chest, watched his nipples as they contracted, then stroked along his flat abdomen, pushing her fingers into the steely wall of his muscles before gliding relentlessly downward.

She liked the freedom of touching him as she pleased. The need to touch and the privilege of doing so combined to give her a heady sense of triumph, as if she had accomplished a task long desired but always denied. Like him, she thought she had wanted to make love with him for a long time.

"I love touching you," she whispered fiercely, intensely, as passion rose in surging waves within her.

Sean touched her temple and her hair. "Not as much as I love your doing it." He caressed along her thighs, learned of her readiness. "Again?"

"Please," she requested politely. "If it's not too much for you," she said saucily, secure enough in his arms to tease him.

"I think I can rise to the occasion," he said, laughing at her impudent grin. They made love again, slowly, leisurely, giving each other the deepest pleasure they had ever experienced.

Finally it was time to get up.

After they dressed, they went in search of food. Marietta and her husband, Jean, were in the modern kitchen having a cup of coffee. The housekeeper served them breakfast in the morning room, which was on the east side of the house, facing the sun. The room was warm and cheerful. Other than casting a quick glance at the two of them, Marietta was the same brisk housekeeper that Kim had seen the day before. Inside, Kim felt that everyone should be able to see that she was different—softer, dreamier... happier.

"Grape, of course," she said later, looking in the jar of jelly after eating her eggs.

"Of course," Sean said.

They laughed as if they shared a wonderful joke. After eating they walked through the woods to the north of the house, stopping often to look at some particularly colorful leaf, to admire a mushroom or to steal a kiss. At last it was time, and they set off for Paris at midmorning.

Sean drove her to her hotel, then to the airport. There he held her hands behind her so that he could bring her tightly against his chest. He kissed her once, a long kiss of goodbye.

When he lifted his head, he smiled regretfully. "If we do this much longer, then everyone is going to know exactly how I feel when I step away from you."

"It's those lascivious thoughts," she advised him worriedly. "You really must learn to control them."

He laughed at her pretended concern. Her face was a pale oval in the dark cloud of hair. He touched her under her chin, bringing her gaze to his. With one finger he stroked the smooth skin there, remembering how she had felt all over.

"May I call you the next time I'm in New York?" he asked with sudden seriousness.

She had wondered if he would ask, and what her response should be. She remembered all the months of antagonism between them. They were still the same people. He had some fixed ideal in his mind of a sweet, gentle woman he would someday find and love. She was as determined as ever to make her way in the tough world of fashion and retail. "I think it's better if you don't."

She saw the anger forming and waited, her thoughts crystal clear as to their future. During the drive back to Paris, she had formulated them carefully.

"Mind telling me why not?" he requested, his tone calm and ominously quiet.

"You could get to be a habit that's hard to break," she replied evenly, her gaze never wavering.

A grin started at the corners of his mouth. "And that would be so bad?"

She quickly shook her head. "An affair would be difficult at best. Our worlds overlap occasionally, but not often. What happens when you arrive in town only to find I've just left to handle some problem in, say, my Florida store, even though I knew you were expected?"

"Then I wait for you, or we make it another time." His shrug said he couldn't see the problem.

"You would be furious," she concluded for him.

"Just as your other lover was?"

She ignored the question. "We're not lovers, Sean. We acted on an impulse at the château, but it was for one night only. Neither of us wants a commitment." A smile brightened her face all at once. "We'd undoubtedly have a flaming quarrel and end up not speaking to each other. Think how awkward that would be for Martin and Mary when we met at their house. We agreed to be friends. Let's leave it at that."

"Is that an order, General?" he asked, so softly she was almost alarmed by his great calm. She knew she had seen the anger, but all traces of it seemed to be gone now.

"Yes."

"And if I refuse to follow it, what will you do then? Make me your prisoner? Hmm, I think I might like that." He was teasing her, and here she was, trying to be pragmatic and adult about the whole thing!

"Really, Sean—"

"Really, Kim," he mocked gently. He rubbed a finger over her cheek and stopped to pat the tiny mole near her mouth. "I see I'm just going to have to use the fatal family charm again," he decided with a sigh.

"I'm not going to get involved with you," she declared firmly. "I haven't the time or the energy."

"Last night was pretty strenuous, I'll admit, but don't you think we'll adjust?" he inquired.

She saw that he was enjoying himself. Of course he was. He was a man who loved a challenge. That was exactly what she was to him—a battle to be won.

"You don't like me, remember?" Her chin lifted a fraction.

He considered her statement. "You're bossy and used to getting your own way, but I think I can handle that."

Her denial was serious. "I'm not really bossy. I give orders at work because I *am* the boss, but I don't tell my friends what to do. I do have opinions and I voice them, just as you do. You just don't like it because I don't agree with everything you say." She gave him a defiant look. "Especially about the man-woman relationship. And *that's* why we shouldn't get involved. Our views are worlds apart. I'm not at all the sort of woman you want and you know it!"

"I've changed my mind." His voice dropped to intimate levels. "I want you very much."

"No." She could be stubborn, especially when it was for the good of both of them. He was too engrossed in the magic they had shared at the château to realize what he was saying.

He didn't say anything for a long time, then with a shrug he stopped trying to change her mind. "The General has spoken." He saluted, but with humor, not anger.

After a minute of debating whether she should trust his easy acquiescence, Kim nodded approvingly. Sean obviously realized that while he found her sexually attractive, he had no deep feelings toward her, that an affair between them would be meaningless and he didn't want that. Neither did she. She wasn't sure what she felt for him, but she wanted more than casual encounters at odd moments in their busy lives. Yes, a clean break was definitely the best way.

She smiled at him in understanding, touched his cheek once, then briskly walked out on the jet way without looking back. When she was seated on the plane, her gaze became hazy as her thoughts went deeply introspective.

Closing her eyes and resting her head against the seat back, she relived the night she had just spent. In his arms she had discovered she was a very passionate woman. He had found depths to her that she hadn't known existed. But what female wouldn't respond to a man like him with everything in her? He was the most gorgeously masculine male she had ever met, and he had made her feel truly female. She would never forget him.

No regrets, she had told him. She opened her eyes and sat up straighter. No regrets, she promised herself.

"SO TELL ME what happened in Paris," Layna demanded. Her husband was working late, and she was helping Kim clean out her refrigerator and cupboards the night before she left for Australia. This was the first chance they had had to get together and really talk since Kim's return. Kim had spent long hours every day at the salon.

"Nothing. I saw the usual shows and the same old people—"

"Not that," Layna interrupted. "What about Sean? Did you see him?"

"Yes, briefly."

"How briefly?"

Kim sighed loudly. "How do I manage to acquire such nosy friends?"

"You came back from France with a look in your eyes that, well, that was different," Layna persisted.

Kim frowned. Surely she wasn't that transparent. Besides, she wasn't moping over Sean Stevenson. Not at all. She was just restless. Every autumn she went through a down period when her obligations had been met and she hadn't yet started on the next project. "You're seeing things," she teased lightly.

"Did you sleep with him?" Layna asked bluntly.

"Yes," Kim said. She had to laugh at the look of astonishment on her friend's face. "You asked."

"Yes, well, I wasn't expecting that answer. I assumed you'd hold him at arm's length the way you do most men."

Kim started talking nonstop. "I'm looking forward to the trip, now that I'm committed to it. I've gotten all the details taken care of at the salon, I think. Rafe can take care of anything that comes up in the design house, and the manager can take care of the store."

"Are you changing the subject?"

"Yes," Kim said firmly. She continued, "I hope to get some really good ideas in Australia, a whole new line for fall, something unusual."

"Who is this person who wrote you?"

"Sean's aunt, Mattie Copeland. She's a widow who owns some department stores. I have no idea what she's like, except her letter was very enthusiastic about my coming."

"I think it's a wonderful opportunity," Layna said firmly. "Maybe you'll get over your moodiness while you're away. Tell the truth, aren't you the teeniest bit excited about going?"

Kim considered. "Truthfully, yes, I suppose I am. I've always liked to go places, see new things."

"Maybe Sean will come for a visit while you're there." Once Layna got an idea, it was hard to steer her away from it.

Kim shook her head. "No, we decided not to see each other again, other than as friends meeting at Martin and Mary's house. I suppose I'll see him there once in a while."

"If you're invited to his family home . . ." Layna suggested.

"Mary said Sean and his father quarreled years ago. They see each other on family occasions, but his father won't ask him to return home and Sean won't volunteer. If the father is as stubborn as the son—all evidence says he is—then I doubt if they'll ever get together permanently."

"That's sad, isn't it? I mean, who have you got if you haven't got family?" Layna asked thoughtfully. "What did they quarrel about?"

"Everything, according to Mary. The final straw came when his father tried to force Sean into marrying the daughter of the owner of the ranch next to them. Apparently everyone was for the match, except Sean. He refused to let anyone interfere in his private life. His father threatened to disinherit him. So he left and made his own fortune."

She wondered why anyone, knowing Sean, would try to tell him how to run his life. He was not a man who could be coerced. Surely his father knew that. She frowned in sympathy for the son and wondered at the father's obtuseness.

"Don't frown. You'll get wrinkles," Layna advised. "How old is he?"

"Sean? Thirty-three."

"It's definitely time he was married."

"He hasn't found another woman like Mary." Kim smiled, remembering his declaration about caring and betrayal.

"Mary? Mary as in Mary who's pregnant, married to Martin and lives in a country house with a kid and dog? Is he in love with her?" Layna's lips pressed together in indignation, giving her the puckish appearance of an elf who had eaten a sour pickle.

"Not in love, but he likes her type."

"The clinging-vine type," Layna concluded.

"She isn't a clinging vine. I don't think Sean would want one. He wants a more . . . traditionally minded woman, I think. Someone like you, in fact. You're warm and supportive and understanding, sensitive to other people's needs. He definitely doesn't want someone whom he calls the General."

"Is that what he calls you? The beast!" Layna immediately became indignant on Kim's behalf. "Just because a woman is successful and can make it on her own without having to depend on a man for every crust she puts in her mouth, some men have to say snide things just to protect their own fragile egos."

Kim started laughing.

Layna looked kind of sheepish. "Well, that does get me riled up. But Sean didn't look the type to need his ego bolstered by any false sense of dependency on a woman's part."

"He isn't," Kim said. "Enough of Sean Stevenson. My problem is getting packed and out of here tomorrow."

"I hope this means you're ready to climb out of that rut you've dug for yourself and discover there's a world besides KT Fashions out there. Not that your designs aren't super," she hastily added, "but there are other things in life. You're too wonderful to be wasted."

"Layna, you should hang out a shingle and go into psychotherapy," Kim suggested, trying to stifle her giggles. "You're marvelous for my self-esteem."

"Thanks. Speaking of independent females, where is that wandering mother of yours? When will she be coming home?"

"Not until spring. She wants me to meet her in California for Christmas. I think I will."

"You're lucky, getting to travel so much. I'm just livid with envy."

"With envy you turn green," she reminded her friend.

The next morning Layna promised to water the ferns and to leave the cactus plants alone. "Not one drop of water, I promise." The last time she had cared for Kim's plants, she had drowned the prickly desert specimens.

"Thanks. I'll see you after the holidays." She hopped in the taxi and was on her way to the land down under, home of the kangaroo, koala and platypus. And birthplace of Sean Stevenson. She couldn't help but speculate: Would he appear there as he had in New York and Paris?

6

KIM, IN SPITE OF her churning stomach, watched as the plane approached Sydney. For the first-time visitors the pilot pointed out that the city had been founded on January 26, 1788, as a penal colony. It was the first settlement on the new land.

Far beneath the plane the Tasman Sea flowed calmly, then rose to meet them as they banked slowly and dropped from the sky. The land jutted eastward into the sea and a beautiful arch joined the north side of Sydney Harbour to the south side. Beyond the bridge was the controversial opera house, which looked like seashells poised delicately in the air. A few minutes later they landed at the airport south of the city and deplaned.

"Miss Troussard?"

The man who spoke to her was dressed in dark slacks and a white shirt. While his clothing was not a uniform, Kim instinctively realized he was an employee sent to fetch her.

"Yes," she replied.

"I'm Thomas Keetie. Mrs. Copeland is waiting in the car. I'll take you there. If you'll give me your claim tickets, I'll collect the baggage." He had a very definite Australian accent with broad *A*s and nasal consonants that were almost gone from Sean's speech.

She handed over the tickets. "Thank you."

He turned and started off at a smart pace that had her hurrying to stay with him. Outside a luxurious auto waited at the curb. Her escort opened the back door for her, and she climbed in. He slammed the door and dashed off.

"Did Thomas rush you dreadfully?" a soft voice inquired politely. It had a touch of resignation about it, as if the speaker had long given up on persuading Thomas to slow down.

Kim turned her blue-brown eyes to her right and looked into a smiling pair of eyes that were close to the same shade as Sean's. This was undoubtedly Aunt Mattie.

The woman had reddish-brown hair that was darker than her nephew's and contained a liberal dose of gray. She was stylishly dressed in a silk dress of pale aqua with several strands of pearls around her throat. Kim guessed her age to be around sixty, maybe a bit more.

"Hello. I'm Kim Troussard," Kim introduced herself and stuck out her hand. The hand offered for her clasp was slender with lovely tapering fingers adorned with several rings.

"I'm so glad to meet you. Everyone calls me Aunt Mattie or Mattie," the other woman suggested, leaving the choice up to Kim.

"My friends call me Kim, Mattie," she replied, placing them on an equal footing without presuming on a false kinship.

Well, so much for the amenities, Kim thought, settling back into the plush seat. She was beat. After some twenty-odd hours of flying and taking antiairsick pills every four hours, she wanted only a hot bath and a bed.

She was groggy, disoriented and not inclined to be sociable.

Sensing her distress, Mattie spoke soothingly, "We'll soon be at the hotel. You can rest for a couple of days before we get started. My husband and I used to fly to London each fall, and I know the trip is dreadful."

"That's okay," Kim quickly said. "I'd like to start first thing in the morning, if you don't mind. I want to see your setup and get an idea of the project."

Mattie laughed delightedly. "Oh, you're just as Mary described you—beautiful and brilliant. I know this is going to work out perfectly."

"You know Mary Holden?" Kim asked, surprised.

"Yes, I met her in France earlier this year. A lovely couple, she and her husband, aren't they?" Sean's aunt barely hesitated for Kim's agreement before she rushed on. "Shall I send Thomas for you at nine in the morning? Is that soon enough to get started?" The twinkle in her eyes indicated a developed sense of humor. She seemed quite composed, even bossy, Kim thought.

When Thomas returned, he drove directly to the hotel and efficiently made all the arrangements for Kim. He and Mattie saw her to the elevator before they left.

Once in the two-room suite, Kim headed for the bathroom. Using some bath salts provided by the hotel, she luxuriated for ages in a tub of steaming water up to her chin. Her thoughts kept going to Sean's aunt. The woman wasn't quite what Kim had expected.

Sean had painted a picture of a woman inexperienced and naive, but Mattie Copeland seemed a contradiction. She had been the picture of cosmopolitan composure. Kim couldn't figure her out. Oh, well, it didn't matter. She would only be here a short time.

KIM GOT RIGHT DOWN to business the next morning when Thomas delivered her to the main offices of Copeland's Apparel. With notepad in hand she wrote down all that Mattie told her had been accomplished thus far.

"Okay, let's go to the boutique," she said an hour later when she thought she had the full scope of the project in mind.

Copeland's department store was at the harbor, part of a large shopping area known as The Rocks, which consisted of historic buildings that had been restored to use. As Thomas held the car door open for them, Kim reacted to the brightness of the sun and the springtime ambience with a lift of her spirits. The day was pleasantly warm, so she didn't need a jacket, and a slight breeze ruffled the feathery leaves of the acacia tree, which, Mattie explained, was also called a wattle tree.

Nibbling on her lower lip, Kim recalled that Sean had once mentioned the wattle tree in telling some boyhood story about his youth in Australia. She realized there were many things she recalled about him from their coincidental trips to their friends' house. And many more from their sojourn in France. A sensation of prickles ran over her skin. She was thinking entirely too much about him since she had arrived in his homeland.

Following Mattie into the large, two-story department store, Kim pushed Sean out of her thoughts and analyzed the merchandise displays as she went past them. Each department seemed well organized and smoothly run as far as she could see.

Off to one side of ladies' wear, a small room completely lined with mirrors formed the boutique. It wasn't open yet, and a screen blocked off the entrance. The two women stood inside and glanced all around. A clerk was busy transferring casual blouses from a rolling rack to a circular clothes bar called a "round."

"How many rounds do you have?" Kim asked.

"Twenty."

"Great." That would provide a good selection for browsing. The wall displays were attractively done with clothing hung on closet poles, which were suspended by chains attached to hooks in the ceiling. It was a mobile arrangement that allowed for many combinations. The mirrors added light and distance to what was actually a tiny space. The room had a more "with-it" appearance than the other part of the store. It would attract the modern, casual female it was designed for.

"What do you think?" Mattie asked, a proud look on her face as she waited for Kim's reaction.

"This is perfect," Kim said, with unstinting approval.

Mattie flicked some invisible dust off a jacket. A half smile spread across her mouth. "I thought I would set up a table over there for the food and serve it buffet-style. Then the models could come out of the dressing area over there." She pointed to the four steps that went up on a platform that had several doors opening off it.

"You're going to have the show here?" Kim asked, frankly horrified at the idea.

"Yes. What's wrong with that?" Mattie asked.

"Well," Kim began, trying to be tactful, "for one thing, where will your guests sit? At the price you're charging for the show, people will expect something better than milling around with a plate in their hand."

"It is for charity," Mattie said. She didn't appear to be taking the criticism too hard.

"Yes, but..." Kim paced back and forth. She snapped her fingers. "Did you say you had a restaurant in here?"

"On the second floor."

"Could we use it? That would mean we'd have to close it to the public for that one day." She looked questioningly at Mattie.

"What a good idea. We'll put up an announcement the week before and run it in the newspaper ad."

"Let's go see what it looks like."

Kim started off, and Mattie fell into step beside her, a pleased smile on her face. Poor woman, she was probably relieved that Kim was there to take over the problems of planning and executing a charity fashion show. And there were always lots of problems, Kim had found from personal experience. As the day progressed and her list of things to do grew, that conviction didn't change.

Returning to her hotel after nine that night, she threw off her clothes, put on her nightgown and fell into bed. Once there she didn't go to sleep but brooded over the happenings of the past month. She wondered where Sean was.

The restlessness returned, and she was troubled by the slight sense of depression she had experienced recently. That night with him had shown her that something was missing from her life. She pictured herself years from now. What would she become? A business executive? She rejected that image. It was part of her, but so was the artist who loved design and texture and color. And so was the woman who wanted it all—success and recognition, passion and love.

CARPENTERS WERE BUSY building a dais for the models to walk out on before they strolled among the guests at the restaurant tables. Trudy Pennington, one of the country's top models, was instructing the debutantes on how to walk, stand and turn in order to show off to advantage the styles they would be wearing.

"It's all going so well, isn't it?" Mattie asked Kim, stopping beside her while Kim pored over her notes.

Kim studied Sean's aunt. There was a puzzle about this woman that she couldn't figure out. She was so pleased with Kim's help, yet Kim had the sneaking suspicion she could have done as well on her own.

During the past two weeks Kim had come to like and respect Mattie Copeland. The older woman was a tireless worker and had a wonderful way with people. The debs just adored her and called her Aunt Mattie with obvious affection.

It sometimes seemed to Kim that Mattie was acting a part she had chosen to play at this particular time, that she wasn't nearly as helpless as she seemed. That didn't make sense. She depended heavily on Kim to make decisions, insisted on having her advice for the simplest matters and always deferred to her opinion. Mattie seemed to find her adviser delightful and stayed with her every possible moment, chatting guilelessly about whatever came to mind.

Kim now knew the family's history from the day the first settler had come over from England. She also knew that Mattie worried about John, her brother and Sean's father, because the doctor had warned him to ease up a bit and he hadn't. "He works much too hard for a man approaching seventy," she had confided. "He needs Sean, and I think he's ready to admit it if somehow we could nudge him a bit. He's mellowed since Sean left home."

"That's good," Kim had replied noncommittally.

"My brother was foolish," Mattie had continued, her expression pensive. "He wouldn't let Sean try the innovative techniques he learned in college. He wouldn't buy the vineyard in Barossa Valley in Australia that Sean was interested in. He wouldn't finance the gold mining operation. And then to interfere in his personal life! Sean had no choice but to seek his own fortune."

"He succeeded," Kim had mused. "His vineyard in France is one of the best, and his partnership with Martin Holden is expanding its line of products rapidly."

"Have you known the Holdens long?" Mattie had asked.

"I've known Martin all my life—our families were friends—but I didn't know Mary until they married. Now she's one of my dearest friends."

Mattie had smiled sweetly. "Yes, she's a wonderful girl."

Kim grinned to herself. She knew she could never emulate her friend's charming ways: she was too outspoken and impatient. Mary listened graciously when others talked, and while she had an impish humor at times, she was the soul of patience in her dealings with people. Kim held Mary in high esteem and was glad Mattie liked her, too.

Kim had also learned that Mattie lived at Channel Downs, the family cattle and sheep station several hundred miles from Sydney, most of the year now and used the corporate penthouse when she needed to stay in town.

When everyone left for the day, Kim stayed on, checking over her lists and consolidating them into one master plan. Mattie had tried to get Kim to accompany her to a friend's home for dinner, but Kim had declined. She liked the quiet of the office. Because it was Saturday, the place had emptied fast, and she could work without interruption.

After finishing she decided to walk to her hotel. The evening was pleasant, and she stopped to eat on the way. It was dark when she returned to her room, greatly refreshed. The telephone was ringing. She dashed for it.

"Hello," she said breathlessly.

"About time," a deep voice said. "This is Sean. Has my aunt been working you overtime? I've been calling for hours."

He had no need to announce himself, she thought. She would recognize his voice no matter how long since she last heard it.

"Is something wrong?" was her first thought.

"Yes." His tone dropped to husky levels. "I'm not there with you."

She recovered her poise instantly and laughed. "Is that what you've called thousands of miles to say? Where are you?"

"New York. I've been here, then back to France again since I last saw you."

"Ah, the busy tycoon," she quipped, stealing his expression.

His chuckle caressed her ear, and she pressed the phone tighter to her. "How's it going with you? You got the troops whipped into shape?"

"Yes. I've worn out two cat-o'-nine-tails, but things are clicking right along."

"When is the big event scheduled?"

"Friday, a week from this coming Friday."

"I think I can make it."

She was silent for a moment. "Here?" she at last managed in a squeaky pitch.

"Mmm-hmm. I have an experimental station up in the Northern Territory and plan to go there sometime toward the end of next week. I should be able to finish my business and get down to Sydney by Friday, I think. If not, I'll see you Saturday."

"I won't be here," she said. "I'd planned to fly home over the weekend." There, that was decisive enough.

"Don't," he said. "Don't leave until I see you." His voice was like liquid velvet, so seductive and cajoling she could feel herself going soft inside.

"We agreed not to see each other again," she reminded him crisply, determined to be practical.

"We did?" The drawled question was full of surprised innocence.

She felt a quick flash of anger at his teasing. "I won't be here on Saturday." Her tone was prim.

"Then I suppose I'll just have to make sure I get there in time for the fashion show," he murmured. "Maybe I can talk you into a private showing like the one I had at your house. That thin gold thing was unforgettable."

She suddenly saw them as they had been that morning she had discovered him asleep on her sofa. So much had happened between them since. A longing grew in her for the quiet intimacy of shared laughter and companionship. Someday she would find the man who would want that with her, all of it, and they would fall in love and marry. She would wait.

"Sorry, I didn't bring it," she said coolly.

"Too bad." He paused, then, "So long, Kim."

"Goodbye, Sean." She tried to put the same finality in the words as she had when they had parted in the Paris airport.

"LET'S GO WATCH Trudy put the girls through their paces," Kim suggested to Mattie late the next week. "I want to be sure they understand the importance of timing." She glanced around, saw that everything looked fine—only one week before the fashion show and the official opening of the boutique—and led the way to the restaurant.

During the practice Mattie was called to the telephone in the office. "You'd better come, too," she told Kim. "If it's about the boutique, you're better prepared to handle it than I."

It wasn't. The call was from Thomas Keetie. John Stevenson had been taken to a hospital near the huge cattle ranch. Thomas thought it was a heart attack, but not a terribly bad one.

"I've got to go home," Mattie said as soon as she hung up.

"Of course," Kim said sympathetically.

"You've got to come with me." Mattie clutched Kim's arm, her gaze imploring.

Kim felt sorry for her. She seemed so distraught. "You won't want me in the way. I'll take care of things at this end. You just go and take care of your brother."

"No, no. You don't understand." Mattie clasped her hands together and paced the room. "Really, I need you, Kim. John can be so difficult...." Her voice trailed off.

"Well," Kim stalled, torn between pity and a desire not to get involved with this family any more than she already had.

"Please, Kim."

She remembered Sean saying the same words. How did a person refuse such an entreaty without coming across as an insensitive clod? She sighed. She had agreed to help his aunt; she would keep her word, no matter what it entailed. "I suppose Trudy can handle the rest of the details since everything is planned, arranged for and flowing smoothly."

"Then let's be off," Mattie said briskly. She picked up the phone and made reservations on an afternoon flight for both of them. Kim was impressed with her control.

FROM THE AIRPORT they went straight to the hospital in the small town that served the scattered cattle stations in the area. Since it was dark, Kim didn't gather an impression of the place, except that it seemed to consist of one main street and several side streets. The population couldn't have been more than a few hundred. The hospital was a clinic with an emergency operating room and a dozen in-patient beds.

John Stevenson wasn't in any of them. He was standing by the window in the waiting room, fully dressed and ready to go.

"I told that fool not to call you," he grumbled when Mattie, Kim and Thomas, who had picked them up, rushed into the room.

"It's a good thing he did," Mattie said sharply. "What are you doing out of bed? Where's the doctor?"

"Here I am." A young man in a white jacket strolled in. "You can have him. He won't listen to me."

"Is he all right?" Mattie asked, concern evident in her voice. John Stevenson snorted impatiently.

"Just some angina and shortness of breath," the doctor answered. "See that he slows down, or the next time will be serious." He was as matter-of-fact as if they were discussing the weather. "He's got to hand over the reins to a younger man."

"I've been running my business for forty years. I don't need some cocky jackaroo who thinks he knows everything taking over."

The doctor shrugged good-naturedly. "Suit yourself. What kind of flowers do you want for your funeral?"

Kim, after her first shock at the casualness of the medical personnel, relaxed and enjoyed the controversy. She caught a wink from the doctor and grinned.

Sean's father ignored the question. "You ready to go?" he demanded, looking at his sister. Mattie nodded.

"Is he supposed to take any medicine?" she asked.

"Just the usual if he needs it for pain." The doctor saw them to the door and watched them drive off.

Kim sat silently in the back seat beside Mattie and wondered why she had let herself be persuaded into coming on this senseless trip. Obviously Mattie could handle her brother, and he wasn't bad off. He sat in the passenger seat in front of her, and she studied the back of his head. His hair was all white. His son's would probably look the same, thick and wavy, when he was seventy, she thought.

Had she come because she had wanted to see Sean's home? Yes, she finally conceded. Of course, she had wanted to help Mattie if the woman needed her, but deep inside she admitted she'd wanted to see this place, the roots from which had grown that magnetic, forceful man who had induced a passion in her so wild that it had been almost frightening. She closed her eyes, and for a moment it seemed as if she could feel his lips on hers.

"Oh, by the way, this is Kim, Sean's friend," Mattie added. "This soft-spoken gentleman is my brother, John."

Kim said hello to Mr. Stevenson, and he asked if she was the dress designer.

"Yes." She was surprised that he knew about her.

"Welcome to Channel Downs." John Stevenson sounded sincere. He asked about her trip and questioned the women on the grand opening, displaying the same charm that was so attractive in his son.

When they arrived at the station, Kim was delighted with the house. It was large and set on a rolling lawn. The inside was comfortably laid out with both formal and family rooms. The furniture and decorations blended wonderfully.

"It's lovely," she said, gazing at a painting of a small stream wandering through a stand of trees.

"A Streeton," Mattie said, smiling fondly. "One of the first artists to capture the quality of the light and the nature of the eucalyptus trees. Your room is this way. I know you're tired after that plane ride. It isn't usually so rough."

Kim went gratefully to her room.

The bed had a wonderful feel to it. When she peeked under the sheet, she saw it had a sheepskin mattress cover, fleecy side up. It was like lying on a cloud.

Reflecting on another strange day in her life, she wondered if this was going to be the norm. Since the day she had run into Sean in her New York boutique, her life hadn't been on an even keel. She considered what she should do.

Tomorrow she would return to Sydney, she decided. In six days the fashion show would be finished, then she would put all this behind her, just as she had done with the other events in her life that had hurt her. She paused to consider her choice of words, which struck her as overly dramatic.

Making love with Sean hadn't hurt her, nor had coming here to help his aunt; she couldn't, however, shake this restlessness that had seized her for some reason and wouldn't let go.

Usually when she was involved in a project or was traveling and thinking hard on new ideas—as she often was at this time of year—she quickly got over any dissatisfaction she felt with her life. This year it didn't seem to be working. Was it because of what had happened at the château? Was that the cause of the agitation of body and spirit that haunted her?

Sean could never be a part of her life, she reminded herself ruthlessly. They had been attracted to each other, they had felt a need to explore each other more fully in intimate ways and they had acted on the impulse. It wasn't a thing she could explain, but she couldn't let it upset her life.

KIM SIGHED, comparing the peace here to the bustle of the city. It was alluring, even if it was an illusion. She knew that life on a cattle and sheep station must have its harsher moments, but just now she couldn't detect any.

She and Mattie were sitting on a sunny patio, enjoying the quiet of the morning. Thomas and Mr. Stevenson had left them only moments ago to take care of some work in the office.

A worried frown contracted Mattie's brow. "Those two stubborn men. I'd like to crack their heads together."

Kim was startled by her companion's vehemence. "Thomas and Mr. Stevenson?"

She thought the men had been cordial to each other, as well as to the two women, during breakfast. True, Mr. Stevenson struck her as a person who would put business first, but Thomas seemed much the same. Perhaps the rancher and his right-hand man had had a disagreement.

"No, John and his equally stubborn son." She sighed angrily. "John won't ease up. He'll drop in his tracks first. But if Sean was here to take over..."

"Would his father let him assume control? Sean is used to managing his own business without interference. He wouldn't take arbitrary orders from anyone." Kim knew his nature well enough to say that with confidence.

"Well, if we were here to ease the transition?" Aqua eyes met Kim's stare.

"I won't be here," she stated swiftly and determinedly. No way was she going to get involved in this affair! "Why don't you call Sean and tell him his father needs him?"

Mattie smoothed back her hair in one of her quick, habitual gestures. Kim realized the older woman wasn't a nervous type; instead, she simply had a large measure of energy that she kept under strict control. She also had an active, astute intelligence that Kim admired very much, but that didn't mean she was going to get drawn into any nefarious plot.

"I've tried that before. My nephew wouldn't believe me. If you were to call, tell him—"

"That wouldn't work." Kim shook her head.

"You saw for yourself John's condition. In spite of the doctor's caution, he'll work himself into an early grave. He really wants Sean to come home, but he's too proud to ask. If you told Sean that, he might listen to you."

"Mr. Stevenson should call." Her relationship with Sean didn't invite the type of trespassing that Mattie was suggesting.

Mattie looked sad. "My brother is stubborn, so is my nephew, but I love both of them. It's a bit of a go to get either of them to change his mind on anything."

Kim appreciated the understatement. It was more than a "bit of a go." It was a major act, rather on the order of a miracle. Of course, if his father did die from overwork, Sean would hate himself. She knew he would.

"But I'll try once more with John." Mattie cast Kim a shrewd glance. "We could split the labor, you know. I'll work on John, you tackle Sean."

A long silence stretched between them. As Mattie gazed at her with a look of appeal in her eyes, Kim could feel herself being persuaded into participating. It was so hard to say no, especially if Mr. Stevenson was as ill as Mattie implied. And she had heard the doctor's warning. That being the case, could she sit idly by and not let Sean know?

Finally she shrugged in defeat. What did it matter if she made Sean angry? It was for his own good. "All right," she heard herself say.

Mattie beamed. "I know that between the two of us, we can move mountains."

Kim laughed. That was an apt description of the task.

"Now we'll have to find Sean."

"He should be in Australia," Kim said, earning a surprised glance from Mattie. "He called me last week and said he had some business at an experimental station."

"Wonderful. I had no idea he was in the country. He usually keeps me informed. Did he give you the number?" At Kim's negative shake she said, "I'll write it down for you." She left to find paper and a pencil and returned soon with the information, handing the note to Kim with an encouraging nod. She went back into the house to tackle her brother.

After Mattie went in, Kim sat in the sunlight, her mind replaying the conversation. Had she let herself be persuaded because she wanted to talk to Sean again? The faster beat of her heart didn't provide the answer she wanted.

Worried about what she should say to him, she gazed at the blue haze of flowers surrounding the branches of a jacaranda tree. Beyond that thorny wattles grew along a fencerow. The land on the other side of the fence was grass and shrub covered. Cows in shades of russet and brindle, a sort of tawny gray, dotted the fresh green of the fields.

She liked this land of deserts and wide plains, where a person could see forever and could ride for days without meeting another soul. Perhaps she was a hermit in her heart of hearts. A longing to ride out and explore stirred her blood, but she couldn't yield to it. She had a phone call to make.

Gathering her courage, she went into her bedroom and sat down at the delicate satinwood desk and picked up the phone. "I'd like to place a person-to-person call to Sean Stevenson," she said much more calmly than she felt, and read the number off.

While she waited, she perused the guest room given to her. It was painted a pale peach, and rugs covered the hardwood floors. An armoire and dresser matched the bed. Lace curtains were tied back to let the warm summery air blow through. It was hard to believe that winter was approaching back in New York when everything here was bursting with new life.

"Stevenson."

How like him to answer with the one word, curt and to the point. "Sean, this is Kim."

His surprise was almost palpable. "Hello," he said, his voice softening. Its seductive timbre sent a frisson down her back. She was more susceptible to him than she had realized. "Funny, I was just thinking of you."

"You were?" A brilliant question, she mocked herself.

"Yes. Last night and the night before and the night before that . . ." His voice trailed off into laughter.

She had to speak seriously to him. "Sean, there's a problem here," she said firmly.

He was instantly alert. "Where are you? In Sydney?"

"I'm at Channel Downs. Your father is ill. It's his heart." Kim licked her lips nervously while she waited for a response from him. For ten seconds there was only the crackling of static on the line.

"Did he ask you to call?" he demanded, the earlier warmth gone completely.

She couldn't lie. "Not exactly. Your aunt—"

"Ah, Mattie. I should have known."

His sardonic tone convinced Kim that a stretching of the truth was the only way. "No, you don't understand. He asked her to send for you. I volunteered to make the call so Mattie could stay with your father." Well, that much was true, although not in the manner she implied, as if the man was hanging on the brink. "Your father wants you to come home," she said, rushing over the words. Lying to Sean could be a very dangerous thing.

Silence again.

"How serious is it, Kim?" His concern was reflected in the quiet tones.

This she could answer truthfully. "The doctor told him if he had another attack, it might be the last. Your father has to take it easy and regain his health, but he won't turn over the operations of the ranch to anyone. You might have to use a little force," she suggested. "He's talking to Thomas right now about business."

"The stubborn fool," Sean exploded.

The pot calling the kettle black. "Yes," she agreed.

"Which hospital is he in?"

A tricky question. "He insisted on coming home. Your aunt has his medication."

There were several muffled curses from the other end of the line. "I'll be there as soon as I can." He paused. "I look forward to seeing you again."

"I really should be getting back to Sydney. It's only six days until the show—"

"I need to talk to you. I'll be home tomorrow. Come to the airport with Thomas." Sean heard the demand in his voice and tried to soften it. "Please," he added. This was not the way to handle a woman of Kim's ilk. She gave orders; she didn't take them, not willingly. And she obviously wasn't as anxious to see him as he was to see her. Just hearing her voice warmed his body by several degrees. She wasn't a soft, clinging woman, but she sure as hell was a woman.

"All right," she agreed, curious about why he wanted to see her. She wanted to see him, too. "What time?"

"If I can make all the connections, I'll be on the six o'clock plane. Tell my father that, will you?"

"Uh, yes." Kim would let Mattie handle that part. She suspected she would have her hands full with Sean when he arrived. "Well, goodbye."

"See you tomorrow evening," he replied.

When she hung up the phone, Mattie knocked at the open door and stepped inside. "Did you have any luck?"

Kim nodded, feeling very tired all at once. "He's coming in tomorrow night. How did it go with you?"

"John said—" her voice assumed a gruff tone "—'This is the boy's home. He's always been welcome here.'" She grimaced. "But he refused to call him, and he wouldn't give me permission to do it in his name."

"I told Sean that his father had asked for him."

Blue-green eyes met blue-brown ones.

"We're probably in trouble," Mattie said. She tried to look worried, but there was a suspicious tremor about her lips.

Kim experienced that puzzling sensation that said here was something to be figured out if she only knew what and where to start. She tilted her head and studied Mattie. "You aren't the least bit worried, are you?"

Mattie patted Kim's shoulder affectionately. "I have faith that you can handle any situation. You're one of the most capable people I've ever met. I've learned such a lot during the time you've been helping me."

"Thank you," Kim said.

"Like most women, I let my husband make all the important decisions. It seemed only fair. He provided our livelihood. Did I tell you he was poor? He worked his way through school and started his first store in a little storage room off his parents' garage."

Kim nodded that she remembered the story. In fact, she thought she knew everything about the family.

"Yes, well, it left me at rather loose ends when he died."

"Did you ever think of remarrying?"

"No, that isn't the way in our family. We mate for life and only once. Sean's mother has been dead for more than ten years. John would never consider another in her place."

A sudden sadness descended without warning on Kim. She wondered how it would be to be loved that way, so totally and so endlessly. No man had ever loved her like that.

Disconcerted by the rush of emotion, she stood and brushed her hands together briskly. "Shall we go for a walk? I'm fascinated by the country around here. I'd like to explore it."

"Why don't you rest today and let Sean take you around when he gets here? He can explain things so much better than I."

"But, Mattie, we need to get back to Sydney soon."

"Trudy has everything under control. I spoke to her just this morning. You know, she's thinking of retiring from modeling and wants to work in retailing. Do you think she would be a good manager?"

Kim nodded slowly. She was fast reaching the conclusion that she hadn't been needed at all, neither in town nor on the station. Mattie was perfectly capable of running her business.

For the rest of that day and the next she was kept busy with small tasks that left no time for brooding or planning a departure. As she dressed to ride into town, a distance of more than an hour's drive, she wondered if she shouldn't pack her suitcase and head back to civilization. Something warned her that the wide open spaces of Australia were proving detrimental to her heart.

7

SEAN HAD HIS LUGGAGE in hand when he stepped off the plane. He spotted Kim at once, standing by the car next to the control tower, and experienced the strong rush of blood through his veins that the sight of her induced. Just thinking of her produced a sharp ache in him.

Seeing the firm set of her mouth and the tilt to her chin, he knew she was determined to deny their attraction. He admitted their reactions to each other were exasperating and her arguments against an involvement were sound. But not insurmountable.

It was true that their worlds rarely overlapped; that was easily fixed. He could base his operations in New York just as well as in France. Neither indulged in casual affairs, but to ignore the tempest between them was to play ostrich. It didn't go away just because they wanted it to.

And her assertion that she wasn't the type of woman to appeal to him? She was headstrong and independent, she followed her own inclinations and argued for her opinions voraciously, but the fact was that no soft, sweet woman he had ever met had stirred so many and such conflicting emotions in him.

From the first time they met, Kim had had the ability to drive him from anger to laughter to passion, all within a few minutes of coming on the scene. His smile was rueful as he approached the two waiting for him. What was he to do about her? He knew what he wanted to do. It was obvious a no-holds-barred affair was the only way to get her out of his system.

Could he persuade her to that way of thinking? He warmed to the thought of the challenge.

Walking up to them, he shook hands with Thomas, then turned to her. "Hello, Kim. Thanks for coming." He saw surprise light her eyes. A gentle approach worked best with her, he surmised. Could he maintain it? He felt anything but gentle around her.

"Hello," she returned in the same self-possessed tone he had used. In reality she wanted to rush into his arms.

When she climbed into the back seat of the car, Sean followed her. She had assumed he would sit in front and talk to Thomas about the station. He settled comfortably beside her, taking her hand and holding it between both of his, and began to question her. "How do you think my father is? It must be bad if he finally decided it was time to send for me."

Kim hated herself for the worry in his expression. She had put it there. "He's not bed-bound," she said, trying to reassure the son who had come on a moment's notice to his father's side. But of course he would do that, she realized. Sean was that type of man. If needed he would come, no matter what his personal feelings were. "It was a warning, not an attack."

"I understand." He looked relieved.

While their driver efficiently wove through the sparse Saturday-evening traffic, Sean cupped a hand around Kim's cheek and brought her startled face up to his. He kissed her.

"Ahh," he breathed, "but I've been wanting to do that for days. I was going to write you."

"Why?" she asked, retaining her poise with difficulty.

"To invite you to my place after you finished the show."

"Sorry, but my time is accounted for right up to the next New York show in the spring," she said. He seemed bent on an affair with her. So why not take what fate offered? a part of her whispered.

"Well, plans can be changed for a good cause," he said, close to her ear. His lips touched her lightly. "I haven't been able to get you out of my mind. Have you thought about us?"

She laughed raggedly. "I think that's an unfair question."

"A loaded question," he whispered. "Very definitely loaded. With TNT." He kissed her again, and her response was immediate and wild with desire.

No fair, her heart said with each beat. *No fair.*

Against her will her lips parted, and he plundered the moist richness of her mouth, his tongue probing, seeking, demanding that she answer his passion. She did with everything in her. When he at last drew back, they were both shaky.

"God, Kim," he muttered. "I've never known anything like this. You're a rage in my blood."

Kim smoothed her hair with trembling fingers. She hadn't been sure what to expect from this meeting, but it certainly hadn't been this declaration of need. Her eyes went to the impervious Thomas, who was listening to the radio as he sped along the nearly empty highway at a very fast clip.

Sean chuckled. "Thomas won't save you."

"I'm not sure I want to be saved," she retorted lightly.

He leaned his head against hers for a moment before speaking to Thomas. "How's the station going?"

"Fair," Thomas answered. "We've had several good rains, and all the channels are brimming. We've moved the cattle over to the spring pastures."

"What about the sheep?"

"The valley is flooded, but we got them moved to higher ground. The lambing was poor this year. I think it's a mistake to keep sheep at the Downs. Should move them down south."

"Sheep can't handle the rough country that cattle can," Sean explained to Kim. "They need closer watering holes. By fall the channels will be mostly dry, and we'll have to wait for the next rains to refill them."

"I see," she said, assimilating the information. "Does it ever snow here?" she remembered to ask.

"Why do you think we have the Snowy Mountains?" he teased. "Yes, we have winter, spring, summer and fall just as you do in the States."

"Except that they're the opposite of when we have them."

He gave her a long look that she couldn't interpret. "Yes, opposites," he said, then he resumed talking to Thomas.

He's wondering about us, she thought. She was the opposite of what he wanted in a woman, yet he wanted her. Troubled by the conflicting emotions she was experiencing, she remained silent while the men talked for the rest of the ride. By the time they arrived back at the Downs, she thought Sean had a comprehensive view of everything involving the station.

MATTIE MET THEM at the door and threw her arms around Sean. "You're here," she said in a choked voice. Kim felt tears enter her own eyes.

"Yes," Sean said, hugging his aunt. "Where is he?"

"In the study. We put dinner back for you. We should probably eat," she said as if she thought they needed the civilized ritual of the dining room for this momentous meeting.

"I'll speak to my father first," he said decisively. He walked toward the study.

Mattie grabbed Kim's arm and forced her to follow. Thomas gave Kim a sympathetic glance before carrying Sean's luggage up the steps.

"Dinner will be ruined if we don't eat now," Mattie hurriedly spoke up. She clearly was determined to postpone a private conference between the two men as long as possible. Perhaps a delay would lessen the tension, Kim mused.

Mr. Stevenson came out of the study. He stopped and perused his son. Kim felt her heart skip as the two men silently appraised each other. Such a waste, she thought, her eyes going from one to the other. They were so alike in their pride but also in their inherent strength and gentleness. Together they could be an invincible team. What a tragic waste of love.

"Hello, Father." Sean was the first to speak.

"Sean," the older man said with a nod.

Before Mattie could say anything, the two men went into the room and the door closed behind them.

"Will they quarrel, do you think?" Kim asked. She was worried about Mr. Stevenson becoming upset.

"Probably. But Sean will be careful," Mattie decided. She led the way into the living room. "John will have to hold his temper because Sean will be cool and polite. My nephew is one of the most temperamentally controlled people I've ever known."

"Didn't Mr. Stevenson ever let Sean make a decision? I mean, Sean isn't exactly a wimp."

They laughed at the image.

"Oh, yes, Sean would go his own way. He would listen to John and then go out and do what he had originally planned. It made John furious when he found out. Of course, Elizabeth was alive to keep the peace in the early years."

Kim slipped off her shoes and drew her feet up on the sofa. "What was she like?"

Mattie stared thoughtfully into space for a long time before answering. "Sean worshipped her as only a young boy can adore his mother. She was beautiful, with blond hair and big gray eyes that always seemed surprised and delighted by the world. She was warm and loving and all the best things a woman can be."

"You loved her, too."

"Yes, she was my best friend. I brought her home from school on a visit and she never left. John wouldn't let her." Mattie smiled at some fond memory. "He married her within a month of meeting her, but he had already claimed her as his. They just took one look at each other and that was it."

"How romantic," Kim said quietly. "Were there ever any other children?"

"A boy, stillborn. He came before the doctor could get here, and John had to handle the delivery. Elizabeth almost died, so John wouldn't hear of another child."

It was like living on a frontier, Kim mused. A family had to survive so many tragedies that could rip it apart. As far as she could tell, though, there was no reason that Sean and Mr. Stevenson couldn't make it. She was sure they wanted the same things if they could just learn to give a little.

While she and Mattie talked, she kept glancing toward the hall. The conference between father and son was taking a long time. An hour later Mattie suggested they may as well eat. "I'll have the cook send something in for the men," she decided. They each went to their own room shortly after the meal.

SEAN STUDIED THE ROOM as the older man walked to his desk and sat down. The scene was so much like others from his past that he felt as if he had never left. The desk, the brown leather chairs, the bookcases, the worn woolen carpet—all were the same. He breathed deeply of the air; it smelled of wax and furniture polish and the occasional cigar Mr. Stevenson smoked.

"So you're back," Mr. Stevenson announced.

Blue-green eyes flicked rapidly to the center of the room, alighting on eyes the exact same shade. "Yes."

"I suppose Mattie called and told you I was dying in order to get you here. Did you come in hopes of claiming your inheritance?" Mr. Stevenson's hands clenched on the chair arms, but that was the only sign of emotion he displayed.

The question would have been ludicrous had it not been so insulting. Anger ruffled briefly over Sean's face like a wayward wind over a pond surface. "I've plenty of money of my own, and there's less hassle getting it than waiting for you to kick off," he responded with deliberate calm. He had learned the virtue of iron control from the man he faced across the room. "I was told you had sent for me."

The surprised jolt that raced through the older man couldn't be suppressed quickly enough to remain hidden. "I'm still capable of running my own affairs and of picking up the telephone when I need to use it. Mattie shouldn't have—"

The lines tightened around Sean's mouth. "It was Kim who called. She said the doctor gave you a warning and that you needed me." He paused. When there was no reply, he turned toward the door. "I can see I'm not welcome here. Sorry to have disturbed you." He started out.

"Wait!"

The two men stared at each other, each trying to see through the defensive walls of love and misunderstanding and pride that were identical in father and son.

"This is your home, boy," Mr. Stevenson said gruffly. "I've never denied you the use of it. I told Mattie you were welcome to live here anytime you wanted."

He rose abruptly and went to a window, staring out at the night after pushing the curtain aside with a hand that trembled a little as he lifted it.

Sean studied his father, noting the sloping line of his shoulders. Although he had seen the older man once or twice a year at Mattie's penthouse, it hadn't been the same as seeing him here, where his strength and dominance had been the prominent thread of their lives.

There was a frailty in the tall, thin frame that hadn't been there seven years ago when Sean left home. The muscles weren't quite as firm, the flexibility of sinew and solidity of bone weren't as sharply defined. It was as if everything he remembered about John Stevenson had blurred slightly with the years.

Pictures snapped into Sean's mind: those big hands picking him up after a fall from a horse and searching gently over him for broken bones; that broad chest offering comfort to a small boy's woes; those eyes detecting a lie from a hundred paces or giving a smile of encouragement without letting on that they thought a fellow needed it.

Emotions buried under the debris of growing up and becoming a man, feelings hidden by a wall of control as two strong men contended for supremacy began to make themselves felt. Once this man had loomed taller than any other in his eyes. Once the son had followed his father's orders without question. When had that devotion faded? When he had wanted to follow his own ideas, he answered truthfully. Nothing had changed between them along those lines.

But he could see that his father needed rest. He would stay and do what he could . . . for as long as he could.

"If I stay, what will the arrangements be?" he asked.

John Stevenson turned and drew himself up slowly, proudly. "You can take over the day-to-day operations. You'll be in charge."

This was a big concession coming from John Stevenson, who had made every major decision concerning the station for more years than his son had been alive. Sean nodded, recognizing the effort it had taken for his father to go that far. "I'll start tomorrow."

"Who's going to look after your other businesses?" Mr. Stevenson wanted to know. "The wine and import business, the gold mine, that station in the Territory."

Mattie again, Sean realized. His aunt had seen to it that each man knew what the other was doing. She had been the one who insisted that Sean come to the penthouse in Sydney for Christmas those first lonely years, bringing him and his father together the third year on neutral turf. That had become the family tradition since then.

"I have competent managers," Sean said coolly. "I let them do their job. I mostly troubleshoot nowadays."

"Can you trust them?"

"Yes."

Mr. Stevenson nodded, not entirely convinced that a person could control his holdings without being right on top of them.

Sean smiled grimly. Already he could see the battles looming on the horizon. If he was going to be in charge, he was damned sure going to give the orders. That was the first thing his father had to realize. "If you feel up to it, I'd like a rundown on the operations. How far along are you with the shearing?"

For the remainder of the evening they talked station business, pausing only once to allow the cook to bring in a tray for each of them. They resumed the discussion immediately over plates heaped with thick slices of beef and mounds of vegetables, all grown on their own land.

At ten-thirty the men left the study. Mr. Stevenson went to his quarters on the lower floor. Sean lightly ran up the stairs. One battle had been faced, and if not won, at least it had ended with a serviceable understanding; now for battle number two. This one would be handled differently.

As he walked along the carpeted hall, his expression subtly changed. When he reached Kim's room, he entered without knocking and closed the door silently behind him.

KIM DIDN'T CHANGE from her slacks and sweater to her gown and robe. That would have made her much too vulnerable. She sat down in a chair and leafed through a magazine while she waited for Sean to appear.

When he finally did arrive, it was almost anticlimactic. Her nerves had been strung so finely for so long she felt the keen edge of relief at finally confronting him. She had decided to be calm and conciliatory. Maybe.

He stood in the middle of the room with his feet planted apart and his hands jammed into his pockets. "You lied," he said without preamble.

"Yes."

She had wondered what his attitude would be, whether flaming anger or cold fury. It was neither. His lips were twisted into the sardonic smile he had often turned on her when they met in the past. His eyes were tinged with just a hint of not-quite-dislike but a feeling closely akin to it. So they were back to square one as if the night in France had never happened, nor the husky longing of the phone call, nor the passionate kiss in the car coming home.

"Ah, yes," he said, his smile seeming that much more dangerous due to the control she witnessed behind it. She suspected he wanted to throttle her. "I don't like being lied to."

"Would you have come home otherwise?" Kim forced a quiet into her voice she was far from feeling. He was ominous, standing there so still.

"You might imagine my surprise when my father took my presence as a sign of my desire to make amends and his surprise when I explained I had returned at his request," he continued as if she hadn't spoken. With one step he was suddenly beside her. "The General just has to take charge, doesn't she?"

The nickname had once been somewhat insulting, later she had found it amusing, now it hurt.

"I didn't know how else to get you here," she explained. "You're too stubborn to listen to reason, so I had to use other tactics. A life-or-death strategy seemed the only solution." She refused to apologize.

"You could have tried the truth. I see both your and Mattie's delicate little hands in this," he accused. His eyes narrowed, and he paced around the room like a confined panther.

"Then why are you staying?"

Sean cast her a glance that questioned if she was stupid. "Because he's obviously going to kill himself if somebody doesn't take over."

Kim was relieved. "If you realize that, then you must also realize he loves you and wants you here. No, wait," she requested when he started to speak. "Has he let anyone else take over? Your father isn't feebleminded. He knows he's got to let up, but he wouldn't do it until you arrived. Now he's willing to let you run things."

"His way." Sean tacked the words on to her statement.

"If you'll just practice a little tact and diplomacy, he'll come around. At the very least you can listen to him, then do things your own way. You'll be giving the orders, won't you?"

"Yes, but I'm not here to discuss me and my father. We've come to a working agreement. You're the problem as I see it, and my first order of the day will be for Thomas to take you to the airport in the morning."

"That hurt," she said, frowning up at him. She had expected it, but it still hurt. "What I did I did because I thought it was best for you."

The heat accumulated in those cool turquoise eyes. It was like watching an explosion building, and she experienced a tremor in her composure. He would never hurt her physically, but a verbal lashing could be as bad.

Sean moved closer. He ached to reach for her, to shake her until he cracked that shell of icy calm she wore like a mantle about her. He forced his hands to stay in his pockets and his mind to stay sharply clear.

"Stay out of my bloody affairs," he advised. "That's what always irritated me about you. You're so sure you're right. What makes you think you know better than anybody else?"

She allowed herself a moment to admire his self-control. He was the most magnificent animal, a child of the sun god, a creation of Pele, Hawaiian goddess of the volcano. Within herself she sensed her longing for him like a froth of lava bubbles. Once more the whimsical smile passed over her mouth.

"I don't," she said, her voice silvery soft, the way a woman should speak at night with her lover in the bedroom.

Sean quenched the roar of passionate flames that rose to choke him. In her blue eyes with their earth tones mysterious knowledge abounded. She had always understood everything about him, he thought. He had never grasped the pure crystalline structure of her nature, not even after making love to her.

"Don't you?" he asked, using sarcasm to cover a host of other emotions that played like a hidden river in him.

Kim didn't defend herself. She didn't mention that he had asked her to help his aunt and that his aunt had asked her to help in this matter. Instead, she reminded him, "I know *you*. You're not the type of person who takes responsibility lightly, and if you didn't feel an obligation to your father, if you didn't care about him, then why did you come?"

His smile was cold. "Perhaps for the reason he suggested—to claim my inheritance."

"Oh, Sean," she murmured. "Did he really say that to you?" She reached out toward him, her eyes full of sympathy.

He stepped away from her hand. "Save your pity," he growled. "I don't want it. I don't want anything from you. Is that clear?" He glared down at her, sudden fury roiling like a stormy sea in his eyes.

"Yes, very clear." She watched him pace the length of the room. His glance swept over the desk, the dresser, the armoire and the bed before finally settling on her. Slowly the emotions that churned within him changed. She saw the turbulent anger fade and the color of his eyes intensify as if he had just realized where they were and that they were alone.

He came toward her, towering over her with his superior height and strength. "On second thought, perhaps we should make the best of the situation," he suggested without tenderness, his gaze going from the bed to her.

"No."

"You've decided?" he asked very softly.

Kim gauged his mood. He wanted her to challenge him, to defy him. He wanted to overpower her with passion. And he probably could, she admitted to herself, but he wasn't going to know that. She wouldn't give him that much satisfaction. Arrogant male, she thought, experiencing a strong rush of warmth for him.

She smiled brightly up at him. "No, you did. You need meaning in your relationships, remember? Our night in France was an experiment. More than that would be a commitment."

He considered her logic. "Damn you," he said, his expression changing to one of irritation, but no longer menacing.

Kim knew she had won. By reminding him of that night she had brought back the gentleness he was incapable of violating when dealing with the female sex. She watched as he turned and left her room abruptly, then, with a shaky sigh, she went to bed.

"THE VIEW FROM THE AIR is so much better," Mattie told Kim the next morning while they were all at breakfast. Sean had just confirmed he was staying, and his aunt was transparently happy. "Sean can take you up. He wants to look the land over—"

"Check that all the sheep were moved to higher ground," Mr. Stevenson cut in, giving the unnecessary order.

"I have a lot of work to do," Sean said to his aunt. "Kim is leaving this morning. Thomas will drive her to the airport when she's ready."

For a second, just to be perverse, Kim toyed with the idea of staying for an extended visit, but one look at Sean's hard face and rugged masculinity told her not to play games. He was devastatingly handsome in jeans and a chambray shirt, and she was much too responsive to his charm should he decide to use it on her. "I'm packed."

"Oh, no," Mattie exclaimed in annoyance. "This isn't what we planned—" She stopped, realizing she had said too much.

"Planned?" Sean asked, a dangerous quiet in his tone. His eyes flicked between the two women suspiciously.

"I meant I thought we would stay here until Thursday, then go back for the show," Mattie explained.

"I'm leaving today," Kim stated unequivocally.

If she didn't get away from him, she was going to explode. She hated his attitude, as if her intercession in his life had been done with intent to harm rather than to help. Never again would she be so foolish as to get mixed up in people's lives. She had let Sean Stevenson get too close to her. She had let herself care about his happiness. Never again would she make that mistake. Angry with herself, she stared across the table at him, her expression carefully aloof.

"Too right," he said, glaring back at her as if she had defied him rather than agreeing with his order that she was to leave. Damn, but she made him furious! He thrust his chair back and left the house.

Mattie turned to her brother. "He's just like you."

"Humph," he said.

"If you want Sean to stay, you'll have to change your tactics," his sister advised.

The older man's brows sailed upward in shock at the reprimand in her tone, and Kim had to hastily press a hand to her mouth. Her eyes gleamed with approval.

"Is that so?" he inquired in the same tone of understated menace that Sean was so successful at using.

"Yes. You were wrong to try to force him into your way of thinking before. That's why he left. He isn't a man given to hurting those he cares for. In this case, it was easier to leave. Why don't you give him a chance to show you what he can do instead of giving out orders like a feudal despot?"

Mattie mightn't have had children of her own, but she knew enough about father-son relationships. Kim was very pleased with her stand and silently applauded the older woman as she took up for her nephew.

Mr. Stevenson suddenly turned to Kim. "Sean said you were the one who called him. I suppose he told you all his plans."

Put on the spot, Kim answered truthfully, "No, but Martin, his partner in New York, said Sean's a wonderful manager, good with people, good with plans and good at executing them. I've seen him in action at his vineyard. That's where he's happiest, working with the land, studying ways of using it so that it benefits everyone without harming the environment. A ranch, uh, station," she corrected, "is probably his natural habitat."

"As a koala's is in a tree?" Mr. Stevenson suggested with a dry humor similar to that demonstrated by his son at times.

"Exactly." She breathed a sigh of relief. He was taking their advice seriously, she thought.

He sipped the strong coffee and said nothing. Mattie wore an expression of satisfaction, but she, too, remained quiet.

"Well," Mr. Stevenson finally announced, "I've let him take over, haven't I? A tad of thanks on his part wouldn't be astray, would it?"

"But," Kim said slowly, "if you dropped everything and came to a person's aid, would you thank them for the opportunity?" Her steady gaze asked that he honestly consider this view.

Mr. Stevenson studied her. "Bit of a pusher, aren't you?" he summed her up. It wasn't clear if he disapproved or not.

"I tend to speak my mind," she admitted ruefully.

"Ah, yes," he said. He observed her with eyes that were shrewd in their sizing up of people and seemed to come to a conclusion. "I'm sorry to see you leaving so soon. I think I'd like to know you." He even smiled a little as he made this surprising statement.

Kim laughed as the tension evaporated. "I doubt that. I don't seem to wear well with men."

Mattie patted her arm. "You're a lovely person, Kim. These foolish men are blind if they can't see that."

"Yes, well..." Kim shrugged, leaving the thought unfinished. She turned to Mr. Stevenson to voice another point she felt important. "The current business attitude in the States is a revival of the entrepreneurial spirit even in large companies. A business goes stale if new ideas aren't tried out. Even if only one in a hundred succeeds—"

Mr. Stevenson held up both hands, demanding peace. "I'll listen to the boy. But I don't promise to agree with everything he says."

The discussion was over and Kim rose. "If Thomas is ready, I'd like to go now. Mattie, will you be down for the show on Friday?" she asked, digging an antiair-sick pill out of her purse and swallowing it.

"Yes, of course." Mattie escorted Kim out to the car, where the efficient Thomas had her bag stowed in the trunk and the engine running. He took off at once, cutting short their reminders of the last-minute details that each should see to.

When the plane lifted off and headed for Sydney two hours later, Kim watched the land fall away below them. She saw that it was flat, like a great plain, with many water-filled channels scoring its surface. Flying southeast over the Murray River basin, she noted the increasing lushness of the country that gave way to the forested greenery of the mountains. Then they were setting down in Sydney.

When Kim returned to her hotel suite, its silence was haunting. She wished that she'd never met Sean Stevenson and that she hadn't come to Australia to help his aunt. She wished she hadn't called him. Most of all, she wished she hadn't fallen in love with him.

8

"OFF CENTER! I want it off center! To the left, Mike." Kim put her hands on her hips. "To your *other* left," she said as he shifted the floral arrangement to the right. She gave up on verbal orders and helped him move into position the eight-foot stand of lilies that would serve as a backdrop to the stage.

She glanced at her watch. Only thirty more minutes. It was a good thing she had brought her dressy outfit to the store with her. There was no time to return to the hotel to change.

In two hours, three at the most, she would be finished with this job. Her flight back to the States was scheduled for the next morning. Mattie had insisted that she stay for a celebration dinner, although a meal was far down on her list of things to do for the evening.

To tell the truth, she was tired. She felt edgy and out of sorts. Falling in love was neither healthy, wealthy nor wise, she decided, angry because she hadn't been able to foresee the emotion or prevent its happening.

She checked over the dining tables. They were lovely, set with snowy-white tablecloths and napkins and low vases of spring flowers. The waiters and busboys were bringing trays of salads from the kitchen.

Going into the dressing area, which was formed by using silk screens as walls, she found that Trudy had her notes in order and that the models were prepared. The changes of clothing were lined up neatly on rolling racks.

"Nearly time," Trudy called to her.

Kim nodded. "Attention, everyone," she called out. When the models and helpers looked at her, she said, "I'm really proud of what we've accomplished in one short month. You've gone into this with the willingness of professional models. I'll give each of you a recommendation anytime you need one." She paused as the young girls giggled appreciatively. "For Trudy, the store manager, the dressers and all of you who so wonderfully helped out, Mattie and I think you deserve an award for valor."

At this signal Trudy handed around gift boxes containing a necklace woven with tiny enameled hearts in pastel tones, designed by Kim for this occasion. Everyone received a present.

"I'm going to change now," she called to Trudy after the applause and thank-yous died away.

Trudy waved and went back to looking over her papers. Kim turned and headed for the office where she had left her dress. Her eyes collided with turquoise eyes, and she felt as if she had been shattered.

"The farewell to the troops?" Sean asked in a husky voice, his humor overcast with other traits she couldn't name.

In New York he had greeted her in just that fashion, simple words spoken in his deep, quiet voice, and her life had altered drastically from that moment. She ignored the clamoring of her heart and smiled coolly.

"Yes. Excuse me." She brushed by him.

His hand flashed out and caught her arm. She looked down at his strong fingers, then up at him, clearly posting Off Limits signs. He dropped her wrist.

"I'll see you later," he said, a promise in the statement that sent a flash of excitement along her nerves.

She nodded regally and swept out. In the office she slipped a blouse of fresh green over her head and pulled on a pleated skirt of green and blue diagonals on white. She belted a blue sash around her waist and tucked her feet into blue three-inch sandals that made her ankles look delicate.

Quickly she twisted her hair into a loose chignon and stuck a jeweled Japanese pick through it. There, she would do. She was going to stay backstage and help the stage manager and dressers instead of joining Mattie at the table, she decided.

Rushing into the restaurant, which was open only to ticket holders, she spotted Sean sitting at the table with Mattie. She was torn between wanting to go sit next to him and an equally strong desire to avoid him altogether. Love was the most confusing emotion she had ever known. It was nothing like the schoolgirl crush she had experienced with Martin, or the later relationships of her college and career days. What she felt for that obstinate mountain of a man was tempestuous, exhilarating and terrifying.

"Kim, it's time to start," Mattie called.

"I was going to check the back," she replied. Coward!

"I just did. Trudy says everything is fine." Mattie gestured imperiously for Kim to join them. "Come take your seat so we can get started." She was beautifully dressed, impeccably groomed and apparently at ease about the grand event.

Kim reluctantly sat down between the aunt and nephew. She was at once aware of him. It was like walking into a magnetic field. Her skin tingled as if beset with tiny electrical shocks. This adolescent reaction couldn't be love, she decided. It was too ridiculous.

Trudy walked out on the stage and took her place at the lectern, accompanied by enthusiastic applause. "Good morning," she greeted. For better or for worse, the show was on.

They had decided to enlarge the fashion palette by going from morning to evening. The first models strolled out on stage in night attire, moving with lithe grace as they stretched and yawned prettily.

"Nice," Sean commented under his breath. "But not as sexy as that filmy thing you wear. You looked like a sunbeam in it, all warm and golden—"

"Shh," Kim hissed.

"And soft and beautiful," he finished.

She swallowed hard against the lump that was threatening to form in her throat and gave him a frowning glance.

The empty soup bowls were taken away, and a vegetable course with fish croquettes was served. Glasses of cool white wine went well with it.

Sean lifted his glass. "Our local wine doesn't have the elegance that France's has, but it's coming along. The white that we drank at Charente the night we had dinner there was—" he paused to consider "—at its peak."

She didn't want to remember that night at the château. Staying with him had been the height of foolishness on her part. She realized that now, when it was too late.

Deciding that directness was the best means of evasion, she looked at her nemesis and asked in challenging tones, "What does elegance in a wine mean, anyway?"

"It means that the wine has the correct qualities of taste and bouquet, of texture and color. It also means it has a certain elusive quality that is a combination of the others plus something more. . . ." His voice trailed off as his eyes roamed over her face and settled on the tiny mole next to her lips.

Heat rushed over her body, warning of his effect on her. Was he being flirtatious and sexy, or was she just taking his remarks that way? There was still a small wedge of anger in him, she surmised. He hadn't forgiven her for interfering in his life. But there was also the desire. He still wanted her. She could see it in the darkening of his gaze as he studied her.

"Don't look at me that way," she told him, her voice pitched low.

"What way?"

"You know." She gave him a reprimand with her eyes. He only grinned and shook his head as if she was beyond comprehension. Sighing, she wondered what devil had prompted him to attend this show.

Glancing around at the other men in the room, most of whom were also in the apparel industry, she saw that Sean didn't look out of place. He was perfectly comfortable in what was basically a female environment. She couldn't help but smile. The brute would be perfectly at ease in a harem.

The image of him with other women chased the smile from her expressive lips. When a finger touched the mole next to her mouth briefly, she glanced at him again. He was studying her as if trying to figure out what made her tick. If he found out, she wished he would tell her!

Through thin slices of roast beef and potatoes au gratin, through tennis togs and jogging suits and an assortment of evening pajamas, Kim sat without speaking, lost in the turmoil of her inner desires and the practical advice she kept giving herself on the foolishness of falling in love with a handsome redheaded devil who seemed bent on tormenting her with stormy glances from sea-colored eyes.

When the show was over at last, she jumped up and dashed into the back to congratulate everyone on a job well done. When Mattie caught up with her, the older woman was alone.

"I'll meet you in the dining room of your hotel at eight for dinner tonight," she advised Kim. "Can you and Trudy finish up here? I have some other business to attend to."

"Of course." Kim waved goodbye and got to work sorting out the clothing to be displayed in special groupings from those items that were to be returned to their proper racks. After finishing she and Trudy sat in the office and chatted about the fashion industry until the afternoon became evening.

Realizing the time, Kim rushed back to the hotel, took a quick shower and dressed. Just as she picked up her purse and headed out, a firm rap on the door caused her to jump. She peered through the peephole, then flicked off the lock and pulled it open.

"Hello," she said, gazing up at Sean. His dark evening suit was a magnificent contrast to his attractive hair and eyes. "Wow," she breathed, taking in his splendor.

"Same here—wow," he teased, looking her over just as intensely. He became serious. "I need to talk to you."

She wrinkled her nose. "Let's not spoil dinner. Where's Mattie?"

"Waiting for us in the dining room. You're late."

Glancing at her watch, she saw that she was. "Then we'd better go, had we not?" she asked brightly.

He took her arm, and sensation shot all the way down to her toes. In the elevator she eased away from him. When he cast her a sharp glance, she made her expression unreadable as she brought her rioting emotions under control.

"Here she is," Sean announced to Mattie when they arrived at the table.

Kim returned her friend's greeting and responded politely to her enthusiastic report on the fashion show. "An unqualified success," Mattie assured her.

Sean helped Kim into her seat, and the maître d'hôtel presented the ornate gold-scrolled menu, managing to look arrogant and give her a little bow at the same time.

"*That* was elegant," she told Sean, who immediately understood that this was elegance she could recognize. His eyes gleamed with humor.

The problem was that he was just too darned attractive, Kim decided, looking at the menu. And fun to be with... when he wasn't angry at her. Also too virile, too intelligent, too perceptive and too many other things for her to enumerate. Her quick smile came and went, leaving her expression pensive.

Sean tried to figure out the rapid changes that went over his dinner partner. He sensed she would have avoided him if that had been possible; barring that, she had obviously decided to make the best of a difficult situation. Why should she feel awkward with him? They had been magnificent lovers, finding depths and heights to passion that neither had known before.

The stirring in his body warned him from those thoughts. And now was not the time for desire between them. He had another task to perform. After giving their orders to the waiter, he settled back and waited, listening to the women talk about their business.

It wasn't until after the meal and they were sipping an aromatic blend of coffee and cinnamon that Kim knew her time had run out. Sean had something to say to her, and he was determined to say it. Standing, he held out a hand to her, a silent invitation to dance. She accepted.

On the dance floor he folded her into his arms, bringing her snugly against his large, graceful frame.

"You're elegant, too," she murmured, her smile teasing all at once.

"Thanks," he replied. There was a moment of silence while they moved with the music, bodies touching lightly, their hands clasped behind her back. "I'm sorry."

She missed a step. "For what?"

"For accusing you of butting in."

"Well, I did. And I lied," she said truthfully.

"Aunt Mattie explained that she persuaded you to make the call for her." He took a deep breath, and his chest moved against her breasts. "My own stubbornness forced you to lie."

"That's kind of you—"

"Besides, I was angry that you didn't call me for yourself," he continued his explanation.

Her mouth dropped open. "For... for myself?"

His grin was wry. "I wanted you to want me the way I wanted you. When I heard your voice, well, I assumed..."

"You conceited lout," she said. Her smile flashed over her mouth, and his breath was taken by her beauty.

"Mmm-hmm."

He held her closer, drawing her into total contact, and flames erupted inside her. "Sean," she said repressively. The state of his desire was unmistakable.

"Don't fight," he whispered, holding her that much closer.

She laid her head on his shoulder but immediately raised it. "I can't stand by and watch my friends make a mistake if I can do anything to prevent it." Her face reflected her earnest wish that he should understand this facet of her. "There's so much unhappiness in the world, Sean, and some of it is so unnecessary. Like the quarrel between you and your father."

His face hardened momentarily, then he sighed and pressed her against his chest. "He and I are managing. Don't think you can make a habit of ordering my life for me," he warned gently but with a spike of harshness in the words.

"No, I won't. It was only in this one thing, when you were being so bullheaded, and I knew you and your father needed each other—"

"I think we'd better change the subject before we get into another battle, General," he said.

She had to grin at the resignation in his tone. "All right. Thank you for admitting I was right." She just couldn't help tossing in that little barb.

He gave her a scowl, then kissed her right there on the dance floor.

"Sean!"

"Kim!" he mocked. "By the way, my father wants you to come back for a visit. He likes you, he said. I think you remind him of my mother."

"Was she bossy?"

"She was a holy terror," he averred. "She could outmaneuver my father just by batting her lashes at him. Her arguments were illogical, but she nearly always won him over to her view."

Kim laughed softly at the combination of complaint and admiration in the son's voice.

"You're a terror, too, but a logical one," he continued. His lips pressed a fleeting caress onto her temple.

A warm feeling, like being wrapped in a woolly blanket, settled over her. This was the first time he had ever revealed anything this personal to her. Perhaps they could be friends after all.

"Will you spend your vacation with us?" he asked.

"I need to work. I haven't had time to do one sketch," she protested feebly, visualizing how wonderful staying at the station could be.

"You'd get lots of inspiration at the Downs. It's at its loveliest this time of year. I'll take you riding," he offered, ending his argument persuasively. "You'll see kangaroos and Ayers Rock and the Northern Territory. You'll love it."

She wanted very much to go with him. If they spent some time together, a quiet interlude of getting to know each other, who could tell what might happen? Her optimism bounced her spirits skyward as Sean cradled her against him in growing passion. That was a problem that needed addressing, she decided.

Without subterfuge she tackled it. "There could be nothing but friendship between us."

A flicker of disappointment riffled the smoldering passion in his eyes. "No, I didn't think you would sleep with me again."

"Oh? Why not?" She wanted to understand how he had arrived at that conclusion.

"You've made it pretty clear. Once the General gives an order, that's final." He chuckled.

She was somewhat hurt by his judgment of her. He thought of her as an opinionated busybody, which didn't foretell a peaceful future for them. On the other hand, it didn't seem to bother him as it once had. There had been none of the mocking humor in his nickname for her that there had been when he had visited New York on Mattie's behalf, nor the sarcasm of the other night.

How long had it been? Six, no, seven weeks. Seven weeks. So short a time, and yet a lifetime. Her life had changed from the moment she had turned and run into him in her Fifth Avenue boutique. She had been unable to shake off her restlessness or to immerse herself in work to the exclusion of everything else, the way she had done in the past.

The music segued into another slow melody, and she let herself flow into Sean's strength. His hard thighs moved against hers as they glided in small circles, staying in the same spot. His hands, still holding hers in gentle captivity behind her back, pressed against her lower spine, bringing her into the closest possible contact. She sighed as heat seared her.

"It's possible we could have the best of both worlds," he mused aloud, taking up the conversation again. "I mean, we're so naturally great together in bed—and that's no conceit, it's true—our relationship would just have to follow suit, don't you think?" He looked at her as if expecting instant agreement.

She swallowed with difficulty. He was a brute to tease her this way. "We have no relationship."

"*Au contraire*, my fair friend. We have the beginnings of a very beautiful relationship . . . if you'd only admit it."

"No," she said firmly.

"Now who's being stubborn?"

Before she could argue with him, he twirled her around and around, making her dizzy, then guided her back to the table with an arm around her waist. During their conversation she had made up her mind. It was definitely too dangerous for her to return to his home.

"Well?" Mattie demanded. "Did you remember to mention John's invitation?" Her amused glance was skeptical.

"Yes, as a matter of fact, my dear aunt, I did. Kim is—"

"Going home to New York," she interrupted hastily. "I already have my reservation."

A frown settled heavily across Sean's brow. "You just said you would go with us. I have the plane. We're flying out at eight in the morning." He spoke as if his plans were irrefutable.

Kim shook her head, and her hair swished attractively around her face. She had a poignant look about her eyes, almost as if she were sad. "I didn't actually agree, and now that I've thought about it—" and was out of his arms "—I think it would be wiser to go home."

"Wiser?" Sean questioned, his eyes going stormy. "What's wise about returning to work when you obviously need a rest? I think you've lost weight. Don't you think so, Aunt Mattie?"

"A rest is definitely in order," she agreed. "Please do come. John did ask for you, and that's the truth."

"She's afraid she won't be able to resist my charm," Sean said facetiously to his aunt.

Kim flicked Sean an exasperated glance. "I am not afraid of anything, especially international playboys like you."

"International? My reputation is growing." He laughed and tweaked her hair. "Come on, General, say yes, and let's make love, not war, the rest of the evening," he cajoled.

"I'll think about it" was as far as she would go.

After talking business for a while, Mattie decided to go to her room. Sean kept Kim dancing for hours.

"This might be the last time I get to hold you," he said, taking her to the dance floor again. They had danced almost every dance.

"I need some sleep. I have a plane to catch," she said grumpily at three in the morning.

"I'll see that you get up," he promised.

Kim bit nervously at her lower lip. "Sean, I'm going back to New York. It's ridiculous to prolong this agony—" She wished she could call back that word.

"Ah, so you do want me," he whispered in satisfaction.

"Yes." It was so much more than mere *want*. The ecstasy and torture of being in his arms was almost more than she could take. She needed to get back to the security of her home.

"Kim."

Just the way he said her name made her tremble with longing, but she thought their being together was a mistake. They were poles apart in their thinking and their needs. There just wasn't any point to letting this wildness of the blood push them into a position where they would both end up with regrets.

She sighed and lifted her hands from around his neck to cup his face. "Please don't make this harder for us. What would a temporary affair prove? That we succumbed to an irresistible attraction? We've already done that. Let's leave each other with good memories. Nothing could be better than that night at the château. Let's save that and—"

"Shut up," he growled, locking her in a crushing embrace. "Listen, I know it won't be easy, but we can work something out. You can spend your vacations here, and I can get to New York a couple of times a year. I don't want to give you up."

"An affair isn't your way, nor is it mine."

"I'll make an exception for you." He tilted his head to one side, and studied her. "Will you make one for me?" he asked softly, teasing and taunting her with their mutual desire.

She brought her thumbs together over his lips and stroked back and forth across his mouth. He caught one of her hands and pressed a kiss into the palm, his tongue stroking with erotic intensity while his eyes never left hers. She tried to figure out his sudden determination to have an affair with her.

The answer was surprisingly fast in coming. He was a virile, dynamic male who wanted her with a tumultuous desire that hadn't yet been appeased. One night hadn't been nearly enough. She conceded that point, for it was the same with her. But neither was an affair enough, not for either of them. They both wanted more from life than that, she thought.

During the past few weeks she had come to a greater understanding of Sean. He had said he needed meaning in his relationships. She was sure he would eventually grow bored with only passion. And that was the future she found so hard to face, she realized.

She wanted a lifetime with him. She wanted to be loved with the loyalty and intensity that Mattie had indicated existed between Sean's parents. She wanted too much.

"Kim?" He was impatient with her.

"All right," she said.

When he took her upstairs, he lingered inside her sitting room for a long time, kissing her until she was at the melting point. "It's late," she murmured, fatigue wrapping around her like a worn blanket, ragged and heavy.

"I know," he said. When he released her, he touched her reddened mouth with one finger, brushing back and forth across the soft fullness as if he was imprinting the shape and texture on his memory.

"See you in the morning at eight sharp." He left.

Kim didn't go right to bed. Instead, she packed and set out a pant outfit to wear on her trip. When she finally lay down, she stared at the ceiling for a long time.

AT SIX IN THE MORNING Kim was up and dressed. She looked around the suite. Everything packed. Picking up her suitcase and purse, she headed for the door. Like fate repeating itself, someone knocked twice just before she reached for the knob. She peered out the peephole. Sean!

Steeling herself for an argument, she opened the door.

"Ah, good, you're ready," he said. With one swooping motion he threw her over his shoulder and held her in place with one hand while he grabbed her suitcase with the other.

Frantically she held on to her purse and tried to push the streaming hair from her eyes as she was carted off toward the elevators. "Put me down this instant," she demanded. "I'm not going with you. I'm going back to New York."

"You agreed to go last night," he said uncategorically.

"I lied."

"Mmm-hmm, you're getting quite good at that." He gave her a friendly smack on the rear as he stepped into the elevator. "Better watch it, though. It could be habit-forming."

"You said you weren't leaving until eight."

"I lied." He chuckled at her indignant snort. "Here's Mattie. Did you get the doughnuts and coffee?" he asked, showing Kim that he had thought of everything.

Mattie waved a white bag. Bending, she inquired of Kim, "Are you all right?"

"No, I'm not," Kim said. She pushed herself upward with one hand in the middle of Sean's back and angrily tugged her hair to one side and out of her eyes.

"Of course she is," her captor assured his aunt and the bell captain, who was eyeing them nervously.

With no sense of embarrassment—he hadn't the grace to be embarrassed!—he carted his burden outside and dumped her on her feet only to push her into the waiting cab. He gave the suitcase to the driver and jumped into the back with Kim, moving over to make room for Mattie.

"You're crushing me," Kim told him.

"That's not all I'd like to do to you," he said, full of good humor.

"I'll get sick," she warned with a nasty smile.

"No, you won't." He fished a tablet out of his pocket and opened a cup of coffee from Mattie's cache. Kim took the pill without thanking him for his thoughtfulness.

In a short time the three of them were in a two-engine plane, heading across the mountains toward the interior.

"The Australian Alps," Sean pointed out as if he was a tour guide as well as their pilot.

"Some Alps," she sniffed.

"Don't be disparaging," he advised. "Your Rockies may fall down someday."

"Never," she declared firmly.

"Never say never."

His laughter reminded Kim that she had said never to him before and look where it had gotten her—right where he wanted every time. It occurred to her that he had no compunctions about interfering in her life while he inflexibly resisted any such meddling in his.

They arrived at the Downs before noon. Kim, never having flown in a small plane before, looked a bit green around the gills, but she made the trip without becoming ill. When Thomas drove them to the house, Sean carried her bag up to the bedroom she had stayed in before.

He saw her surprise. "Did you think I would whisk you right into my lair?" he asked.

"Yes."

"Disappointed that I didn't?" he murmured wickedly, giving her a look that sent lightning flashes along her nerves.

"I think I won't answer that," she said crossly.

"Maybe I'll charm it out of you."

He put her suitcase down and came to her, his mouth going unerringly for the honey of hers. The kiss was gentle but passionate, showing her all the qualities she had come to expect from this man. She clung to him shamelessly, needing him as she had never let herself need anyone. It was dangerous; it was foolish; it was beyond her to resist.

9

KIM JOINED MATTIE on the veranda at eight the next morning. She didn't expect Sean to be there, and he wasn't. He and his father were on a flying inspection of the southernmost pastures, she learned from Thomas, who joined them for a cup of coffee when he finished his office chores.

"I'd like to go riding. Would that be possible?" Kim asked. She had her sketch pad with her and wanted to do some drawing.

"I'll take you," Thomas volunteered. "I need to get out—"

"Sean will want to take Kim," Mattie stated.

"That's true," Thomas said, nodding wisely after exchanging a meaningful glance with Mattie.

Kim wasn't sure she liked being so obviously labeled Sean's woman. "Do you think he'll ever have time?" she asked, doubting that he would.

"He'll make time," Mattie said confidently.

Her prediction came true. At lunch father and son returned from their aerial survey. Sean seated himself next to Kim when they ate. After the meal he tweaked her hair. "How about a ride?" he asked. "Feel up to it?"

"Yes." Her smile leaped to her mouth and stayed there. "It's been several years since I've ridden, though."

"We have a gelding for you," Mr. Stevenson said. "Casper is trail-smart. If you get lost or in trouble, he'll bring you home. Just give him his head."

Some of her pleasure dissolved. "Am I going alone?"

"Not today, but I have no doubt that you will in the future," Sean said, a knowing look in his eyes. "Bring your pad and pencil."

Kim made a face at his broad back as he rose and led the way to the stable. Behind them she heard Mattie say something and Mr. Stevenson and Thomas laugh heartily.

When she and Sean were on their way, her enthusiasm soared as their kite had in Central Park. She felt on top of the world. Glancing at Sean, she thought there could be no companion more handsome or nicer in all of Australia.

"What are you grinning about?" he asked, looking over at her as their horses trotted side by side. The gelding, Casper, was gray and white. Sean's Jazzman was a big brown stallion.

"Why Jazzman?" she asked, ignoring his question.

"He likes to dance around before he gets into the swing of things."

She recalled the horse prancing and pawing and stamping before it had finally obeyed Sean's commands. It was a beautiful animal, and so were the others she had seen in the stable. Australians were as proud and particular about their horses as the Irish, she had heard.

"I want to check out a bore over this way," Sean called over his shoulder as he let his horse out into a run. "Let's give them a workout, shall we?"

"Yes," she shouted. Casper was already pulling at the bit. She eased off, and he galloped after his stablemate.

They ran across the spring pastures, here and there dotted with wildflowers and thorny shrubs. Kim loved the wind blowing against her face and tossing her hair behind her in wild abandon. She felt so free and uninhibited.

Sean picked up the pace when he saw that she could keep up. He gave out a long ululating yell that sounded aboriginal to her and spurred Jazzman forward. Casper stretched his stride and pounded alongside, determined to stay with him. Kim laughed, and she imagined the sound spreading out behind her, like a comet's tail following its source.

They leaped over a small rocky outcrop and then the red slash of a small gully washed out by the early rains. Sean brought them to a halt at a windmill beside a watering trough.

"We have the bores to get us through the dry spells," he explained, checking out the equipment after they dismounted.

"Why don't you call them wells?"

He gave her a scolding glance from beneath his brows. "Because we call them bores," he replied. "The water comes from the Great Artesian Basin. Sometimes we have to *bore* down four thousand feet to reach it."

"I see. Why do you call ranches stations?" she immediately questioned, a teasing light in her eyes.

Finishing his task, he wiped his hands on a handkerchief and came over to her. "Because that's what they are." He hooked a hand behind her neck. "Did anyone ever tell you that you talk too much?"

She considered carefully. "You know, I think someone once did." Her smile flashed up at him. "I threw him into the swimming pool."

"Is that a challenge? Are you going to try to toss me into the cattle trough?" His deep voice echoed through her nerves, its pseudoseriousness belied by the sparkle in his eyes.

She shook her head, feeling herself being drawn nearer to his warm, hard body. "I gave up taking on mountains years ago," she declared wisely. Her heart was hammering against her ribs. She should never have tangled with this mountain of a man. He was winning hands down.

"Don't you know the way to move mountains is one grain at a time?" he murmured. His breath stirred playfully across her lips before his mouth closed over hers with expert skill.

Kim arched upward to meet him as his arms swooped around her body, bringing them into crushing contact. Their bodies moved as one, pressing and swaying against each other with a need that was overpowering. His lips moved at various angles over hers, demanding everything in a kiss. She gave willingly, opening her mouth to him, returning his quests into her depths with searches of her own as she explored him more fully.

"I've missed you," he said later. "I thought one time would get me past this madness, that it would answer my curiosity about us and the hunger we've shared for each other. But it didn't. My appetite is whetted, not satiated."

She pulled out of his arms and stood a few steps away, regaining her breath and her composure. Her need for him was an ache deep inside her. Closing her eyes, she tried to shut out the clamoring of her heart and her blood. It was no use.

"I think we'd better go back," she suggested.

"No, not yet," he said quickly. "I want to take you somewhere. I told you that you'd get lots of inspiration here, and I think I know just the place."

They mounted and rode off. Thirty minutes later he stopped beside a channel and hobbled the horses, then led her up a small hill that wore a rocky outcrop like a hat.

"Oh, yes, this is lovely," she exclaimed, looking out over the country. She could see how the tributaries flowed into one another, forming a giant irrigation system that was entirely natural. "Where does the water go?"

Sean stood close behind her, holding her sketch pad and pencil, which had been stored in her saddlebag. "It flows very slowly toward Lake Eyre. To the west—" he pointed over her shoulder "—is Simpson Desert. Beyond that is Mount Olga and Ayers Rock, all part of the Great Australian Shield. I'll take you to see them," he promised.

A frisson ran along her neck. He sounded so serious, as if it was terribly important that she see the land.

"Now, you get to work with your sketches and I'll do the tea." He handed over her pad and pencils and went back to his saddlebags to get the supplies.

While he started a tiny fire in a solid fuel container used for camping, she sat on a rock and gazed at the landscape. She sighed deeply, contentedly. Although aware of Sean close by, she nevertheless knew a quieting of her spirit. After weeks of troubling questions before finally admitting she loved him, she was, for this moment, at peace with herself.

With a tiny smile trembling on her lips she contemplated what he would say and do if she told him that she'd fallen in love with him. Laugh, probably. She couldn't bear that. Her love was too new, too fragile for clumsiness in handling.

Nothing could come of it, she reminded herself. In a couple of weeks she would be gone, and this interlude of magic would be over. Better to let it die gradually now rather than prolong it in the bittersweetness of an affair. She frowned at the pain that settled like a lump in her chest and reiterated her decision, nodding wisely as she did.

"Here's your cuppa," he said, handing her a tin cup of tea, already sweetened to her taste. He set some cookies on a napkin next to her. Sitting down at her feet, he took a cookie and ate it in two bites while she munched thoughtfully on one.

"It's lovely here," she commented after a time of quiet.

"You haven't drawn anything. Doesn't it inspire you?" He leaned on her knees and gazed up at her earnestly.

Like a small boy who's disappointed that his treasure didn't please his friend, she thought. She held her cookie out to him and he ate it, taking a playful nip at her fingers in the process.

"I'm soaking up atmosphere." She stretched her arms over her head, causing her breasts to press against the white cotton of her long-sleeved blouse.

His hand lifted and cupped the irresistible treat. Her nipple was a hard peak in his palm. Kim couldn't speak for a moment, then she gently removed his hand. He chuckled unexpectedly, and she glanced at him with raised brows.

"I can't help it. I don't think I can be around you and not touch." His grin was wry. "But I'll make a superhuman effort."

"Here, have another cookie." She put one in his precocious hand to keep it busy.

Her body tingled with desire, and she almost gave in and reached for him. Then she recounted all the reasons not to get involved with this cowboy—correction, jackaroo—from the outback. "Is this the outback?" she asked.

"I suppose you could say so, although I think of Western Australia and the Northern Territory in connection with the term." He leaned his back against the rocks she sat on and looked out over the surrounding country. "It's a fair land."

The simple statement told her how much he had missed it. A constriction formed around her heart. This was his home, where he would stay and raise fine sons and daughters to inherit the land. Her home was New York.

Pulling her sketch pad onto her lap, she began to draw, starting with the rocky promontory to indicate the flatness of the plain below and the erosive effect of water through the channels. After a while she realized Sean was asleep.

He must be tired, she thought tenderly, smoothing a strand of his brightly colored hair. He rose at the crack of dawn and tackled the problems of the station without pause until long after dark. Mattie had told her how hard he was working.

"He's just like his father," the older woman had said. "Only Elizabeth could slow John down. She was the only person with enough influence over him to do so. It's the same with Sean. He needs a loving woman to devote some of that energy to."

The words echoed relentlessly through Kim's mind. A loving woman, not an occasional diversion. She sighed and closed her pad. The muse wasn't with her today.

THE DAYS FLOWED into one week... two... the beginning of the third week found her still there. Sean had taken time to fly her out over the desert country. They had flown to Alice Springs and on to Ayers Rock after he conducted some business at a ranch on the way. She had loved it.

Her fingers had skimmed over the paper as she captured one idea after another for a new line of leisure wear. The rusty red tones of the rocks, the brilliance of the sun and the blue of the sky had inspired her to experiment with the color combination of rust, yellow and blue. So far it was a success—at least on paper. The real test would be when she ordered a sample run of fabrics and made the sportswear.

Sean had watched her work and made comments. "Yes, I like that," he had said, approving of her coveralls, which were actually two pieces for ease of removal. She pictured the items in sturdy denim for camping and in silk for lounging.

He had thought that a rather novel idea. "Maybe even a little strange," he had suggested, teasing her while his hand stroked through her hair and his chest supported her back while she worked. When they returned to the station, she found that a letter from her mother had caught up with her.

"I really must leave this week. Christmas is coming, and I promised my mom I would join her when her ship ties up in California," Kim remarked at dinner the next evening. She had ridden with Sean and his men on a cattle roundup all day and was tired but happy.

She had been given the task of counting the beasts as they came through the chutes to be tagged and medicated for worms and various other ailments they were prone to get. It had been fun, and she had felt very much a part of things as she helped out. Sean had seemed pleased to have her tagging at his heels for days, and he often complimented her when she performed some insignificant task. His quick hugs and touches as they worked together added a sort of ecstatic torment to her days.

"I wish you could spend the holidays with us," Mattie said. At a glance from Sean she quickly added, "But of course we understand that you must be with your mother."

"Invite her over" was Mr. Stevenson's practical advice. He seemed to have mellowed a great deal these days and even enjoyed having his son take over. Kim thought it had been his secret craving for a long time. Of course, he still bellowed ferociously at times, but Sean took it in stride and continued with his plans.

She thanked them but declined to extend her stay. Leaving was hard, but the longer she lingered, the harder it would get.

That night she prowled sleeplessly around her room, filled with a longing to go to Sean. Standing by her window, she saw him cross the yard and climb the fence. In the moonlight she watched as he leaped onto a tall horse and rode off bareback. He was as restless as she was. Sighing, she went to bed. Not for the first time she regretted her decision to keep Sean at arm's length.

The next morning she decided it was definitely time to go home and get her life back in order and running smoothly. She had her sketches and ideas for a new line of clothing. It was time to get down to the nitty-gritty details of fashion design.

"Why so serious?" Sean asked when she joined the others out on the patio.

"I was just thinking of work. Speaking of which, why are you having breakfast with us?"

"What a slave driver," he grumbled. "I came back to the house to get you, smarty. Do you want to go?"

"Yes," she answered promptly without asking where. That drew a laugh from Mattie and the other two men.

"Then hurry and eat," her guide advised.

A few minutes later she was astride Casper, trotting after Sean and his big stallion and singing "Waltzing Matilda."

"Don't let Mattie hear you singing that."

Kim looked into blue-green eyes and felt herself drowning. "Why?" she managed to ask.

"That's her name, and the boys used to sing that to her when they came courting. She started using her family nickname and refused to answer to Matilda anymore."

Kim was delighted with this insight into Mattie. She had grown to like the woman enormously. "I'm glad I came here, Sean. I'm glad I met Mattie and your father and Thomas. And I appreciate your showing me your land," she added softly.

The cool aqua of his eyes burned over her for a long minute. "I'm glad, too, Kim," he said huskily.

Passion flashed white-hot between them for a moment, then he spurred Jazzman into a gallop and led the way toward the northwest. After a bit he slowed and told her some of his father's prize sheep had been spotted over that way, trapped in a meadow with water on all sides.

"If they stay, they'll eventually run out of grass, so we need to make them leap off the jump-up and swim over to a pasture near the road. There we can load them onto caravans and take them down to the southern station."

Kim had learned enough to know a jump-up was a small cliff formed by erosion, a caravan was a big truck with two or more sections and the southern station was a smaller ranch that Sean owned down in New South Wales, which was well suited to sheep. Mattie had taught her the family history, and Mr. Stevenson had brought her up-to-date on the ranch.

"Bloody stupid sheep," Sean commented sometime later when they came upon about thirty of them after jumping across a gully filled with water. "My father paid a fortune for these. They're a new hybrid, supposed to have the best wool of any in the world."

"I see. I really like the woolly mattress cover on my bed. It's like sleeping on a cloud," she said without thinking.

His quick, amused glance alighted on her face. "Wait until you've slept on one on a water bed," he suggested softly.

"Is that what you have?" she asked, her imagination offering up tantalizing scenes of his bed.

"Yes."

She couldn't tear her gaze from his. His eyes promised her paradise in his arms, and she knew that's what she would find if she only accepted the invitation that he extended to her with every glance, every touch, every smile. Soon she would be gone, and never again would she know the ecstasy of his kiss. Her eyes filmed with tears, and she looked away.

"Stay here, and I'll drive them over the edge," he ordered.

Jazzman didn't like mixing with the short, fluffy creatures. He balked and shied each time Sean cracked his whip over the heads of the sheep. Soon they were milling in a circle rather than jumping off the cliff into the water. Sean swore and threatened horse and sheep with instant death.

Kim snickered, then burst into laughter as once more the creatures scampered past her. Giving her a look of umbrage, he slid off the excited stallion and handed her the reins. Going into the midst of the animals, Sean grabbed one and worked his way to the edge, where he pushed it off.

A couple of curious sheep ventured near the edge, and he gave them a shove, too. They joined their companion and easily made it over to the grassy meadow on the other side of the shallow runoff. Four or five others went off on their own, and that started the general stampede.

Sean would have been fine if he hadn't stooped to help a lamb over the cliff. Its mother bumped him, causing him to lose his footing. As Kim screamed a warning, he was hit from the opposite side by a young ram who was eager to join the crowd. All of them disappeared over the edge, and the rest of the flock went after them.

Urging Casper to the jump-up, she saw Sean go under and several sheep trample on him as they scrambled ashore. Then she couldn't see him at all, only the white froth of the sheep churning against the water, which had turned opaque from dirt. She screamed his name, but there was no response.

Terror beat in her breast like a flock of frightened birds. She glanced frantically around. There was no one to help. She had to get to Sean. Without hesitation she dismounted and jumped off the edge.

The water was waist-deep for perhaps twenty feet before it grew shallow. She fought her way around bleating sheep until she spotted Sean. He was pushing himself upright when she reached him. "Are you all right?" she asked anxiously.

He stared at her, then back at the cliff where the two horses watched them. He cursed impressively. "How are we going to get back up there?" he demanded.

Kim followed his gaze. "How were you going to get back up?" she countered.

"You were going to throw me that rope on Jazzman's saddle," he informed her. "I was going to climb up using that."

"Oh."

"Now we're stuck here."

"Maybe I could stand on your shoulders and..." Her voice trailed off. The drop-off was too high, and there was nothing for her to grab to pull herself up.

Sean bent down and picked up a rock. He threw it. "Go home, Casper. You, too, you stupid horse." He chucked another rock at Jazzman. Kim wondered if he was going to throw one at her, too, for getting them into this mess. Other than a rapidly purpling bruise on his forehead, he appeared unharmed.

Jazzman danced around, but Casper seemed to know exactly what was expected. He turned tail and thundered off. After a second Jazzman followed.

"Well, we might as well get comfortable. It'll be hours before we're found." He began taking off his boots.

Kim stared as he proceeded to undress and hang his clothing on a shrubby eucalyptus tree. When he was stark naked, he turned to her and noted her astounded gaze.

"The shy tycoon," he murmured. "Take off your clothes, Kim. We'll swim as soon as the mud settles."

She realized she was staring. Turning, she watched the sheep stop at a safe distance from the crazy human beings and start grazing. "No, I'll just . . . wait here in the sun."

"Take your clothes off."

It sounded like a threat. "No, I don't want to." She lifted her chin and glanced disdainfully at him.

That was a mistake. He was heart-stoppingly handsome. His hair, darkened by the water, gleamed like embers in the sun while his magnificent body looked like a statue come to life, it was so perfect in its proportions. She stared as he came toward her.

"Like what you see?" he asked, amused.

She tried a nonchalant shrug. "It's okay, I guess." She wasn't going to let him know how the sight of him made her feel.

He stopped in front of her. His hand touched the pulse that beat wildly in her neck. His other hand guided her fingers to his chest, where she could feel the hard, rapid pounding of his heart. "I like what I see," he told her in a low, sexy voice. "You're a treasure a man wouldn't get tired of, not even if he viewed it nightly."

Looking down, she saw her blouse plastered to her skin. The lace of her bra was clearly visible through the semitransparent cotton. Her nipples stood out in the damp coolness.

"I don't think I can let you go without making love to you," he whispered as he lowered his head toward her.

His kiss was gentle and sweet. It was like getting a morsel after weeks of starving. Kim wanted it all. She was aflame with turbulent desire. Only he could satisfy her need.

"Sean...Sean," she said, calling out to him from the depths of her passion as she wrapped her arms around his neck and pulled him closer. The kiss deepened into total contact. His thighs pressed between hers, and she felt the hard strength of his desire pushing against her.

She would be leaving soon. This one last time couldn't hurt, she assured her heart. Oh, she had to make love with him one more time, she simply had to.

He moved slightly, creating space between them. Leisurely he began undressing her. Her blouse. Her bra. Her sneakers and socks. Her pants. Her panties. He hung everything up on a bush to dry before taking her into his arms. Lifting her, he waded into the water, going out to the waist-deep part before letting her down.

Kim wondered why the water didn't steam and hiss when she touched it. She felt so hot, sizzling.

Taking her hand, Sean started swimming and she followed, stretching her strokes while he shortened his. They stayed side by side. Finding a place in the water that was shaded by a tree, they stopped without any words passing between them, and he pulled her against him, burying her sensitive nipples in the coarse playground on his chest.

His hands explored her body, along her back and over her buttocks, caressing her until she called out with need. Her teeth bit at the flesh of his shoulder while his mouth roamed her neck and throat before seeking her lips.

"We'll probably raise the water temperature by ten degrees," he said with a low chuckle as he nibbled her earlobe.

She turned her mouth to him, wanting his lips on hers and the moist excitement of his tongue joining with hers. He smiled at her eager intensity, his face going tender as he gazed at her. She hadn't yet learned to prolong the ecstasy of love play. She wanted everything at once, like a child let loose in a candy store and told she has only a few minutes to get as much as she can gather.

His mouth closed over hers, and Kim felt an explosion of heat inside as his tongue probed her sweetness. With hands on her thighs he guided her legs around his waist. Anchored to him, she felt his hands glide possessively over her.

He explored her intimately, his touch gentle but arousing. She was caught in showers of sparkles, and then the building of the rainbow began. He stroked her until she cried out, until she was frantic for him. Lifting her slightly, he kissed each breast, his mouth hot on her skin, burning her with his passion.

"I've never made love to anyone like you," he murmured, lost in his own raging need for her. She was fire and magic and light in his arms. "You're burning me up."

He sucked gently, coaxing a wilder and wilder response from her. Kim gave herself up to the rainbow as color swarmed in zigzag patterns behind her closed eyelids. Stroking down his chest, along the taut abdomen, she found what she so ardently desired and guided him home to her.

"Ohh," she breathed as he moved deeply into her. She cried out in little moans, encouraging him with the audible evidence of her need.

"You're so smooth," he whispered, nibbling at her lips, devouring her greedily with his mouth while his body worked its splendor on her senses. "Flame and silk."

"Don't stop," she requested.

"No, I won't," he promised, loving her look of rapture, her movements against him. "You are the most exciting woman. . . ."

The heat built in Kim, flaming in sheets of color through her veins. She couldn't breathe, couldn't think. She heard her voice crying his name. "Sean, my love. Oh, darling, yes, yes." She was shameless in her demands, and he answered every one of them without hesitation.

He plunged into her again and again. His hands stroked her to fever pitch, and his mouth engaged hers in endless play as he made love to her until she could stand no more. With a little cry she caught her breath and held it as the rainbow shattered into bursts of red and gold and slowly faded into sunset. She rested helplessly against him, feeling the pulsing sensation of his pleasure as he gasped and crushed her to him, taking his own release when he was sure she was satisfied.

Kim ran her fingertips through his hair as he rested his cheek against her temple and regained his breath. She couldn't recall ever feeling so tenderly toward a man, or any person, she realized. She drew a deep breath and let it out slowly. So much for her resolution about involvements.

Sean locked his arms around her and waded toward the grassy shore. "It's a wonder we didn't drown," he murmured, kissing the side of her face. He looked around at the rocky ground with its thin covering of grass. "It's too rough to lie down, love."

"That's all right." She stroked his shoulders, unable to stop touching him. "We can sit on a rock."

"I have a better idea." He lowered himself to the softer verge on the side of the stream and let her rest on him.

Kim listened to the beat of his heart and drowsed off for a few minutes. After a bit she began to caress him, exploring the hair on his chest, his nipples and downward to his flat stomach, where his chest hair spiraled into a single line that grew thinner the farther down her seeking hand traveled.

By the time she touched his manhood, he was already swelling in anticipation. Surer of herself now, she was bolder than she had ever been, caressing with her hands and mouth until he gasped with pleasure and groaned with the effort it took to hold himself back until she was ready to join him in the final ecstasy.

When she bent over him, his mouth met hers with renewed energy, and his skillful hands took her on the ever-climbing ride to passion's door. They lingered at the threshold until they were beyond sanity.

"You're wonderful, the best there is," he told her huskily. "Do you know what I've been through trying not to remember what you're like in my arms?"

"Yes, I know." She kissed all across his chest.

"I couldn't forget one minute with you. That night at the château was the dream of a lifetime. This is even better."

"For me, too," she agreed, breathing raggedly as his hands rubbed over her breasts, then along her abdomen. He stroked through the dark cloud of hair at the juncture of her thighs, and she could wait no longer. She moved in increasing abandon, his hands guiding and caressing, helping her find the rhythm and share their mutual delight.

When she cried out and fell helplessly against him, she felt his arms tighten and his body shudder with pleasure. He held her until she could move once more. Carrying her into the water, he rinsed the perspiration from their bodies. Later they dried in the sun and put their stiff, discolored clothing on. When their rescuers arrived, they were ready to return to the ranch.

At the house Sean guided Kim to his room. There they shared a bath before going downstairs. He stayed with her that afternoon, giving Mattie no chance to talk to her alone. Kim wasn't sure she could handle the subtle delight she saw in the other woman's eyes. That night, when they went to bed, Sean took Kim to his room with an arm around her waist.

There she discovered the merits of a fleece-lined mattress pad on a water bed. "I'm going to be sick," she told him.

"No, you're not." He covered her body with his. "You're going to be much too busy to think about that."

And so she was.

THE NEXT MORNING they slept late and went down to breakfast together. Mattie joined them for coffee after she finished talking to Trudy.

"The boutique is doing wonderfully. The racks are emptying faster than they can restock," she said to the couple. Her expression was one of quiet happiness.

Kim patted back a yawn and caught Sean's little grin of satisfaction. They hadn't been terribly interested in sleeping.

"Well," Mattie said to Kim after a brief conversation about the store, "I suppose there's no question of your leaving now." She laughed softly. "It's all working out just as Mary and I planned. When I told her my ideas for the boutique, she said you were the one to give advice on the fashion show. Then we had this simply marvelous idea about getting you two together, and—"

"You what?" Sean asked. His brows jerked together in annoyance as he realized what his aunt had said.

Kim just stared speechlessly at Mattie.

Mattie glanced from one to the other. "When you get married—"

Sean pushed himself up from his chair, his hard gaze going to Kim. He was definitely angry, which wasn't surprising. They had been manipulated by his aunt. Her request for help with the boutique had been merely a ploy devised by her and Mary. And it had worked. Without the influence of their friends around them they had recognized and succumbed to the passion that had existed between them, unacknowledged, for more than two years.

"There was never any question of marriage," Kim said to Mattie before Sean could respond in anger, her enormous control keeping her voice steady. "Sean and I live very different lives on opposite sides of the world. We found, that is, we..." She floundered helplessly, unable to explain the sudden attraction.

He spoke, startling her into silence. "We found we like each other quite a lot," he said coolly to his aunt. "How about keeping your nose out of it...and tell that to your fellow conspirator next time you two get a bright idea, will you?"

Mattie tried to look contrite but failed. Sean frowned at her, then smiled enigmatically. Giving Kim a quick kiss, he chucked her under the chin, winked and left the room.

"Kim, won't you please stay?" Mattie asked, ignoring her nephew's orders to keep out of their affair.

"I really can't," Kim said resolutely. "I must go see my mother." That was a good excuse, a reasonable one, and it caused Mattie to subside.

TWO DAYS LATER KIM PACKED and was driven to the airport. Mr. Stevenson invited her to return when she had time. Mattie waved a somber farewell from the front steps, and Thomas called out a friendly goodbye. Sean was driving the car.

He made small talk on the way and asked about her sketches and plans. She replied calmly, explaining how she would select the fabric and make up samples of her clothes to show the buyers at the clothing marts. "I'll be very busy until late in the spring," she concluded. And if she was busy enough, perhaps she wouldn't think of him twenty-four hours a day.

The past two days had been heaven and hell: heaven because she and Sean had been together every moment, waking and sleeping; hell because she had been aware of the relentless ticking of the clock, marking her final moments with him.

He had been the perfect lover—gentle, thoughtful and attentive, making it clear he didn't hold her responsible for Mattie's and Mary's romantic interference. If, sometimes, she thought she detected deeper emotions beneath the humor and passion, she attributed it to wishful thinking and refused to dream about an impossible future for them.

"Do you have to actually do everything yourself?" he inquired. "Run the stores as well as do all the designs and get them made?"

"Oh, no. I couldn't handle all that alone. I have competent managers and accountants to oversee all the operations. And I have a chief designer plus two juniors and several assistants at the design house. I only work on what I want to."

"And oversee the rest of the business?"

"Yes, that's right." It seemed the strangest conversation to be having.

"Then I guess there isn't any reason we can't get married," he said softly. He stopped the car in the airport parking lot and turned in the seat to note her reaction.

She was stunned.

His expression was caught between resignation to the inevitable and an amused anger that life would work this way. "Well, is there? You can conduct most of your business from here. We can combine our trips when I have to go to New York or France. What do you think?"

"You're joking," she managed to get out.

He shook his head. "I still want you. Now that I've slept with you, had you to myself these past few days, I find that isn't enough. I want it to continue. I think you won't find it easy to give up, either." He brushed her cheek teasingly with the backs of his knuckles.

His words were a pain in her heart. She wanted so much more than passion from him. With one of her quick, enchanting smiles she clasped his hand and held it pressed between hers. Slowly she shook her head. "If we had lived a couple of hundred years ago when women didn't have so many choices, if we could have been pioneers together and lived a life that called for two strong people who could each pull their own weight . . ."

A frown gathered between his eyes as he realized she was refusing. She reached over and smoothed his brow, feeling illogically tender toward him.

"That time is past, Sean. You want me, yes. Physically we're suited, but in all other ways? No. I think that's what's confusing you. You want a traditional wife who will be by your side here at the place you love. I'm not that woman. I wish I were. My dreams and ambitions are located in New York, and that's where I belong."

He chuckled softly, a slightly perplexed look in his eyes. "I admit you're not what I had in mind when I thought of a wife. I wanted a softer, more yielding woman, one who would put me first in her interests, but I'm willing to settle for you, General. Not only do I like you in bed, I've found I enjoy arguing with you. You certainly aren't dull to be around."

His words were both complimentary and hurtful, but they brought home even harder her conviction that he was blinded by the strange, wild passion that they had for each other. She had to be sensible for both of them. "We can't spend all our time in bed, and I think you would soon find yourself longing for a relationship of harmony rather than conflict."

"So you're refusing to even give it a try." A cool anger chilled his gaze. "Then go back to your city and your stores and your designs, but think of this sometimes during the long, lonely winters there," he suggested sardonically.

He kissed her then, a kiss that vented his frustration at being thwarted, a kiss that aimed at showing her what she was throwing away, a kiss that promised the treasure of the rainbow if she stayed. She couldn't.

She had a sense of déjà vu as they said goodbye at the gate. He kissed her once more, a long, lingering kiss that was but a shadow of the passion she knew could erupt out of control between them.

"Goodbye," she said when he released her.

He merely looked at her without speaking.

On the plane she thought about her visit to Channel Downs. She tried to put it into perspective, to be practical about the whole affair with Sean. It had been inexcusable for Mary and Mattie to meddle in their lives like that. Of course, they probably envisioned a storybook ending, but that wasn't possible. They should have realized that.

She relived his anger at her refusal to marry him. She wasn't sure why he had asked, but she was sure of her answer. He was capable of deep emotional feelings, and she wanted to be more than a great bed partner, the mad passion in his life. She wanted to be loved, for herself, for all time, and in spite of her bossy ways. She wanted...

"Oh, shut up," she said, startling the man next to her, who hadn't said a word since takeoff.

10

"YOU'RE RESTLESS AGAIN," Kim's mother commented.

She and Kim were sitting on a bench in their host's rock garden, drinking tea and watching the gardener form intricate patterns in the gravel with a rake. The round dais with its small table and two chairs floated like a lily pad over a pool in which goldfish dashed to the surface and stared at them expectantly.

"Shameless beggars," Kim said, dropping a crumb over the edge of the platform.

"Not going to talk, huh?"

"Nothing to say."

"Your eyes are sad. Only a man puts that kind of misery in a woman." Mrs. Troussard's light brown eyes studied the telling flush that stained her daughter's cheeks.

"Your vision is faulty," Kim teased. "I'm just at loose ends right now. As soon as I return to New York and get back in gear, I'll be fine. I'm anxious to start on some ideas I have."

Mrs. Troussard gazed at an interesting boulder that jutted upward at an angle from the gravel. "Maybe it's time you did something different," she suggested slowly.

"Different?"

"You've made it in the business world—"

"A person has to work hard to stay on top, though," Kim interrupted, wary of where their conversation was leading.

"I've never been an advocate of the superperson, whether man or woman. It's too hard. But I think you can have it all . . . if you go about it right."

Kim was amused. "Mom, what are you talking about?"

"You," her parent answered promptly. "You've made it in your chosen field. No one can take that away from you. But your business is so well organized it can run itself now. Well, can't it?"

"Umm, yes, I guess it can. I have very good managers."

"There. You see?" Mrs. Troussard spread her hands as if everything was clearly explained.

"So what?" Kim asked, reminded of her last conversation with Sean. He had suggested she return to Australia. She waited, amused, to hear her mother's recommendation.

"So you should think of marrying and having your family now. You're over thirty."

"Ouch, that smarted. My own mom telling me I'm getting old," Kim complained good-naturedly.

Her mother sighed in exasperation. "You're determined not to take this seriously, aren't you?"

"Take what seriously?" Kim looked at the vines that climbed the rock wall at the end of the garden enclosure.

"The fact that you're eating your heart out for someone, but you won't admit it."

Kim swallowed hard and breathed deeply, holding on to her poise with an effort. It wasn't like her mother to jump into her private affairs. Apparently she wasn't disguising her emotions as well as she had thought.

After a long minute she said softly, "It doesn't do any good to dwell on it. He and I live on different planets, for all practical purposes. Even if we lived in the same town, it would be the same. Our life-styles are very different."

Her mother gave an unladylike snort. "You're one of the most adaptable people I've ever known, and you have the courage and determination to make your life work on your own terms."

Kim managed a gay laugh. "Thanks, Mom, you're wonderful for my ego, but you might be a wee bit prejudiced."

"Go ahead and laugh, but remember what I've said. Think about it," Mrs. Troussard advised sternly.

"Yes, I will," Kim promised.

After her mother went inside the house, Kim sat on into the twilight, her inner vision fixed on wide, sweeping plains of red gritty soil broken by rock outcroppings and eroded gullies. No use thinking of Australia, she told herself firmly. She had made the decision to put it and all that it promised behind her. She would stick to it.

THEIR HOST IN CALIFORNIA, Richard Matashiwa, was an American of Japanese descent. He owned an import-export business that had supplied various products for Mr. Troussard's many business interests for several years. Mr. Matashiwa's niece, Emerald, was spending the holidays with him, too.

He had gone out of his way to make his guests feel welcome. They had driven into San Francisco to visit the stores. They had put up a tree on Christmas Eve and sung carols in both languages with the fifty or so relatives who had shown up to wish them a Merry Christmas, and the day before he had provided the traditional Christmas feast.

Now, as Kim watched him stand beside her mother, she saw his hand touch Mrs. Troussard's shoulder lightly. Her mother glanced at him, her smile charming, her eyes radiant.

They're in love, Kim realized, dazed by the fact. Why not? her heart asked, sounding wise and superior. She experienced a rush of tenderness toward both of them and had to fight an urge to put her arms around her mom and give her her blessing.

Gad, she was becoming sentimental if the sight of affection between two people could bring her to tears. With eyes that were suspiciously bright she smiled at Emerald, who was part British-American and part Japanese and had startling light blue eyes in a perfectly oval face and waist-length hair that was silky smooth and black. She wrote and illustrated popular children's books on nature.

"Kim, I think I will follow your suggestion. Having a contact to introduce me to the *real* life of Australia will be a plus, I'm sure," Emerald said while aromatic tea was served in cups as delicate as fairy crystal.

"Mrs. Copeland will love having you," Kim assured the other woman, who was twenty-four. On an impulse of perfect irony she had offered to mention Emerald in her next letter to Mattie.

Mattie will love her, Kim thought. Emerald was old enough to be mature, but she still had an endearing enthusiasm for life. Kim felt jaded in comparison. And Emerald was a very gentle person, she noted as the younger woman touched her uncle's arm while explaining her intention of doing a book on marsupials.

Kim recalled that Sean hadn't gotten around to showing her the animals. "Sean will take you into the bush so you can see them firsthand," she told Emerald.

The light blue eyes turned on Kim. "Are you sure he won't mind? I can get around by myself."

Her uncle laughed. "You should have seen the place she lived in when she did a book on the Amazon. It had a palm-frond roof and bamboo walls."

"And bugs," Emerald added with her tinkling little laugh.

Sean will love her laughter, Kim mused. They will have blue-eyed children with dark hair and red highlights. She glanced up to find her mother's eyes on her. Her quick smile flashed over her mouth but didn't linger. Pensively she listened to the conversation as Emerald explained the series she had planned for the land down under.

"That sounds as if it will take years," Kim interrupted.

"Probably. I'll need a place of my own. I was thinking of an apartment in Sydney or Melbourne. Which do you think would be best?" Emerald looked to Kim for advice.

"Oh, stay awhile in each," she said casually. Sean will take one look and keep her at the station just as his father had done with Elizabeth, she thought. Perhaps she should wrap Emerald up and attach a note: To Sean, From Kim. She wondered if he would realize she had sent him the perfect woman. And if he did, would it make him furious that she had once again butted into his life?

In her mind's eye she could see them riding out over the land, stopping for a cup of tea and some cookies and then . . .

Heavens, she was turning into a masochist. The idea of another woman in his arms was hell, simply hell. Her cup clattered onto the table, drawing all eyes to her.

"Uh, this is very good," she murmured. Her voice was husky, and she had to clear it a couple of times. "Very good." She smiled brightly at her companions.

"Kim has a lot on her mind," her mother said. "She has to get back to New York and see about her business. I didn't realize I was raising a tycoon, but I suppose I should have. Her father taught her to invest her birthday money when she was hardly more than a baby."

Mrs. Troussard's chatter provided a cover for Kim to regain her composure. She had to stop thinking about Sean. That was over, and she had too many things to do to worry about what couldn't be, shouldn't have been and would never be again. Realizing her thoughts were getting muddled, she concentrated on the conversation until it was time to go to her room.

ON JANUARY SECOND she walked into her apartment in New York, checked her plants, found them all healthy and turned up the furnace. It was miserably cold outside with a slushy snow on the streets and weather advisories warning against traveling.

Layna dashed over and asked a million questions. They went into the kitchen while Kim made coffee, then returned to the living room to sit in front of the fire.

"Yes, it was inspiring," Kim answered the ones about work. "I have a notebook full of sketches. See what you think."

She pulled the pad out and showed her ideas to Layna, knowing they were safe with her friend and that she would get an honest opinion about them.

"Lovely. Great. Super." Layna's response was gratifyingly enthusiastic. "So how are you?" Her glance took in Kim's evasive shrug and wasn't fooled.

"Fine."

"Very stoic, but a lie," Layna remarked.

"You see too much," Kim muttered, pouring another cup of coffee and taking another homemade brownie from the plate that Layna had brought over.

"When are you going to do something about you and him?"

"I'm not," Kim said firmly. At Layna's disgusted stare she protested, "What do you want me to do?"

"Go after him, honey. Are you crazy to let a man like that get away? Besides, he needs you as much as you need him."

Kim shook her head. "He was attracted temporarily, but I'm not the type of woman he wants for a wife."

"Oh, yeah, the clinging vine," Layna scoffed.

"No, not that, but a gentle woman. One who is softer than I am and perhaps more . . . available," she said for lack of a better term. She smiled suddenly, startling Layna. "I sent him one."

"You what!"

"I sent him a woman. She's perfect for him."

Layna clapped a hand to her forehead. "I can't believe you. I really can't."

"I know, but I did the right thing. He needs a full-time wife, not a fly-by-night lover." She was proud of her control as she stated the conclusion she had arrived at weeks ago.

Layna jumped up. "I'm going home. I never could stand martyrs, self-sacrifice and all that baloney." She threw her coat over her shoulders and stomped out, banging the front door behind her for emphasis.

Kim sat in front of the fire again, her mind a blank, as if she was caught in a vacuum. It seemed the safest place to be at the moment.

THE FOLLOWING WEEKEND she went to visit Mary and Martin and Sammy and the new baby, Althea.

"After Prince Valiant's wife," Mary said with her charming giggle. "Martin was in love with her when he was growing up."

"She's lovely," Kim cooed, holding her godchild on her lap.

Martin lifted the baby in his arms and beamed proudly. "She's the most beautiful baby in the world," he declared.

"And I'm the most beautiful boy," Sammy announced.

"You certainly are," Kim assured him, holding out her arms and sweeping him up when he ran to her. She nuzzled her nose in the fold of his neck, getting a whiff of little-boy scent and talcum powder.

Althea spit up on her father, and Kim watched as he calmly grabbed a tissue and mopped it up. He had once been the most fastidious of men. Love could change even the stoutest heart, she mused.

"Tell us about Australia," Mary demanded. "When is Sean coming back?"

"You are in a heap of trouble, my friend," Kim said. "Mattie let your little scheme out of the bag, and Sean is on the warpath with interfering females at the top of his list."

Mary wrinkled her tiny nose. "Didn't you fall in love even a little bit?" With blue eyes and blond hair she looked the picture of angelic innocence.

"Not a smidgen," Kim lied. Her smile appeared and died on her lips. She thought the weekend would never be over.

KIM STUDIED THE BOLT of rust-red velvet.

"Hey, are you still with us?" Rafe Thurston, her chief designer, inquired sardonically. With his eye patch, black turtleneck sweater and black jeans he looked like a pirate rather than a designer of fabric, of clothing for men and women and of furniture that belonged to the future. Rafe was a multitalented person who had won many awards in the field of art before coming to her.

She looked up, her eyes clearing of memory as she again focused on her work. "Yes, of course." Pointing to the outfit she had designed and had her head seamstress make up in the velvet, she asked, "Do you think it will work?"

"I think it's a terrible idea." At her look of dismay he said, "No, really, I love it. Actually it's a good complement to our sportswear casuals. It fills a void at both ends of the leisure-wear market."

She nodded. "I thought so, too. Our Trailblazer label can be worn for roughing it—"

"Or to fancy cookouts where people pretend to rough it," he added with a laugh.

"Exactly." One thing she liked about Rafe was that he caught on to her way of thinking immediately. They had worked well together from the first day four years ago when he had barged into her office and insisted she look over his designs.

"Why do you want to go into fashion?" she had demanded.

"Because I'm tired of starving as an artist."

"You just had a showing—"

"Where few of my paintings sold. People like to look at them; they don't want to buy. Too grim, too realistic." He'd mocked a popular critic's review of his work, then shrugged. "I want to design clothes for men that are comfortable and practical as well as having more pizzazz."

"I don't do men's clothing," she'd informed him.

"It's time you did." He'd raised one brow in challenge.

"Start your own house. You'll make more—"

"If I succeed. I'm afraid my reputation as an artist will precede me. I want to hide behind your name."

Liking his honesty, she had looked over his ideas and liked them, too. He had proven an invaluable help.

"Rafe, have you ever thought about becoming my partner?" she asked, looking at the striking picture he made. His hair was black and silver, his gaze dark and mysterious. He had a quick intelligence and sudden humor that she admired.

"I thought you'd never ask," he said, a smile turning up the corners of his mouth.

"Well, I am," she said, making the decision definite.

"Okay. Now about the Trailblazers, I want to take a similar approach for men. Also, I think I'll design some camping gear—"

She started laughing.

He paused and frowned at her. "What's so funny?"

"You are. I am." She clutched her sides helplessly. "We just made a deal that should require a slew of lawyers, and we didn't even shake on it."

He grinned. "We can do better than that."

Taking her by the shoulders, he brought her forward and upward, then he kissed her. It was an experimental kiss, one that searched for a response in both of them. It wasn't there. He released her slowly.

"It doesn't work for us. By all logic it should. But it doesn't, does it?" he mused.

"No," she agreed, patting him on the arm in a consoling gesture. "We're destined to be just good friends."

They smiled at each other in understanding. His personal life was very private, but she knew he'd had a serious affair with one of their top models a year ago. When a bigger offer had come along, she had jumped at it, leaving Rafe behind.

He touched her hair. "The big, red-haired guy that all the girls were twittering about during the grand opening?" he asked, knowing at once where her heart was given.

She nodded, tears forming a knot in her throat. It had been weeks. Here it was, the middle of February; she should be over the longing by now. Sean and Emerald might be married, for all she knew. She hadn't heard a word from anyone.

"Well, let's look at the denims," she said briskly, closing the subject. "We'll have our attorney draw up the partnership papers tomorrow."

"Perhaps we should incorporate," Rafe said.

"Let's check out the pros and cons." She was the cool businesswoman, looking at all the angles.

"Right."

They shook hands and got back to work on the real business of creating something that people would want to wear. It was late that night when they finished and went home.

KIM FLIPPED ON LIGHTS as she made her way to her bedroom. She hated to come home to a dark house. She had been meaning to get a timer that would turn the lights on at twilight. Of course, she never remembered it until she was home.

She changed into a fleece-lined jogging suit before returning to the living room to build a fire in the fireplace and go over the mail that had been stuffed into the box on her front porch. There were several magazine brochures from local stores to announce upcoming

Washington Birthday sales. Three letters were in the pack. One was from her mother.

> I didn't say anything while you were here because one, it would have been premature, and two, I knew you saw the situation between us. I hope you will be happy for us. We've been friends for many years, and now to have this other is like a gift from the gods. We plan an early summer wedding here so all his relatives can attend. Will you come? Richard and I will wait for you. . . ."

Kim finished reading her mother's news. It hadn't been unexpected. In fact, she was surprised that it had been this long in coming. They probably had wanted to be doubly sure. She was very, very glad for them. Picking up the phone, she called to tell them so. When she hung up, a smile clung to her mouth.

Opening the second letter, she read that Emerald was very happy, too. She was gathering firsthand material to go in her series of books that would cover all the natural history of Australia. Mr. Stevenson and Thomas were storehouses of useful information, and Sean was a dear—unfailingly patient when he took time out of his busy schedule to fly her to a location where she could sketch the wildlife to her heart's content. They had invited—insisted, really—that she make her base of operations the Downs, and she'd decided to do so. In closing, she thanked Kim for introducing her to her friends, who were now as dear to her as her own family back in San Francisco and England and Japan.

Kim breathed deeply for several seconds before opening the third letter. Her hands shook as she tore at the envelope. Mattie's words were written in her extremely neat finishing school hand.

> You were right to send Emerald to us. She is a perfect guest, adding much laughter to our days as she tells of her experiences in the "bushes"—her term for the experimental station in the Northern Territory. She and Sean spent a week there earlier this month. She came back with a pet rock, a stone polished by the wind in the desert. The aborigines call them "gibbers."

Mattie wrote several pages, telling in detail of their life at the station. When Kim reached the last page, a dried eucalyptus leaf fell into her lap. Its shape reminded her of a short scimitar. It seemed to cut into her heart without piercing her skin.

> I have enclosed a leaf from the tree that grows outside your bedroom window—Emerald's room now, of course—so that you won't forget us.

The letters dropped unnoticed onto the carpet. Kim was no longer in New York in a cozy apartment on a snow-covered street. A blizzard wasn't blowing outside. She was drifting in a shallow stream, securely held by strong arms as she and her lover floated along effortlessly. Her head rested on a broad chest, cushioned by a thick mat of dark hair with auburn highlights. She could hear his heart beating.

His fingers caressed her back. Finally his hands slid down onto her hips. He squeezed, teasing her as they allowed their passion to build and build. They kissed, sinking deeper before he kicked out with his powerful legs and brought them bouncing back to the surface. Laughing, he carried her to the bank.

On a eucalyptus tree their clothing moved seductively with the gentle swaying of the breeze. He placed her in the shade on a bed of leaves, and the scent of eucalyptus rose all around them as he kissed her. . . .

Lifting the leaf, she breathed in its scent as if it could give her what she needed. Dear God, she felt as if she was dying inside. How could the longing for one person be so strong? Where had all this turbulent emotion come from? Why hadn't she found it with someone else? Because she had never loved anyone else like this. It was all-consuming, coloring everything in her life with the pain of wanting that which was out of reach.

Crumpling the fragrant leaf in her hand, she was lost once again in a world of magic. There, beside the stream, the sun was warm and the wind playful.

His hair gleamed like flames in the light, and she touched a strand that wafted across his forehead. Drops of water beaded his tan face, and his blue-green eyes smiled down at her. In them she could read his love. Yes, he loved her. It was clearly there in the stormy depths of his gaze and in the smile that she knew was only for her.

She heard his voice, speaking to her from a great distance, fierce and possessive, "I love you. . .love you."

"My love," she whispered. "My darling, my love."

She had always been his. Always. She had refused to recognize that fact before. In his arms was unbounded joy as well as fiery passion. Together they could work things out. She knew that now.

Lost in her private vision, she saw the couple turn. Dark hair swirled around the woman's shoulders. Sean lifted a handful of the silky tresses and brought it to his lips, kissing the strands reverently.

With a sense of profound shock Kim discovered the woman's hair reached all the way to her waist!

Jarred out of her daydream, she stared at the crushed leaf. Rising, she tossed it into the fire. In less than a heartbeat it had fallen into ashes.

11

"I'M OFF. Don't be too long. I think there's someone out on the street waiting for you," Rafe said, sticking his head around the doorframe to speak to Kim.

"Who is it?" she asked, looking up from the copy of ads that would appear in a national magazine in August.

"Think big," he advised. "Think fire." With a wink he was gone, a piratical laugh echoing down the hall after him.

That could only be one person. It couldn't be. She pressed her forehead to the window so that she could see the street below. It was! She clutched the windowsill. Why was he here?

Feverishly she cleared her desk and locked up. Riding down the elevator, she critically smoothed her pleated skirt and the loose sweater that hung jauntily around her hips. It was not a formfitting outfit, but her breasts thrust boldly against the knitted fabric, and the tan and black colors added a dramatic flare to the style. Casual chic, it was called. She eyed her black leather boots. Sean would probably ask if she were on her way to lead a platoon of storm troopers into battle.

Slipping into her coat as she neared the front door, she wondered what he was doing here. Probably just passing through on business. What business? It didn't matter. He certainly wasn't there because of her. Mattie had probably insisted that he deliver a message.

Knowing her thoughts were becoming scrambled, she opened the door and stepped outside. He was leaning against a lamppost, and his dark blue all-weather coat was dusted with snow. She looked up at the clouds and felt the tiny flakes strike her face. Another storm, the third since the new year had started.

After locking the store, she turned toward him. "Hello, Sean." She waited, her flash of a smile ready for some roguish remark from him about her, him or their recent past.

"Hello, Kim," he said, his voice a quiet rumble.

His eyes moved slowly over her, and flames erupted inside Kim, burning her with the intensity of her longing to touch him.

He took her hand and tucked it into his arm. "Let's hurry. It's cold out here." He urged her to a cab that was waiting, meter running.

"Extravagant," she said, for once doing as he said without arguing, her smile coming and going across her lips.

After he gave the driver her address, he turned toward her, and her heart tripped all over itself as she read the intention in his eyes. Her lashes fluttered down in confusion as his mouth brushed softly over hers, caressing her with gentle touches that were so sweet she wanted to weep.

She turned away and stared out the window, straining for a composure that threatened to slip out of her grasp. It wasn't fair that he could do this to her while he stayed calm.

His hand toyed with her hair until it was time to pay the cabbie and climb out in front of her place. Once in the house, they wiped their feet, then he helped her out of her coat before pulling off his own and hanging both in the closet in the foyer.

"I'll build a fire," he volunteered. In a few minutes the logs were blazing, throwing a cheerful glow into the room and scattering the chill.

"It was eighty-six degrees when I left the Downs," he commented with a smile after finishing his task.

"Perhaps you should have stayed there," she suggested with just the right amount of teasing amusement in the remark. Score one for my side, she thought, taking a seat on the sofa.

He sat beside her and leaned back with a contented sigh. "Ah, it's good to be inside and out of the cold."

"How long had you been standing outside?" she asked curiously. "And why did you wait there instead of coming in?"

"I didn't want to see you with other people around." His stormy-sea eyes flashed a challenge at her. "I thought I behaved with admirable restraint in the taxi. I want more than kisses from you."

Frissons ran in multiple waves along her spine. There was a decisiveness about him that confused her. Just what did he really want?

"Do you have a message for me from Mattie?" she asked, ignoring his statement.

"No."

"Oh."

He grinned. "Well, actually, she sends her love. My father and Thomas send their regards and said to tell you there's a new colt that needs naming. It's sort of a flaming gold color—"

"Vulcan," she said at once.

"The Roman god of fire? Mmm, that fits." His smile became teasing. "Isn't a form of the word used for volcanic eruptions?"

Her eyes went irresistibly to his hair. He laughed at some private joke but didn't let her in on it. Then he merely looked at her in a way that made her heart flutter.

With nothing to occupy her hands Kim clenched them tightly in her lap, trying to still the nervous tremors that suddenly ran through her in a helter-skelter fashion. This was ridiculous, she chided her runaway emotions. She stared into the fire.

His fingers curled into her hair. "Have you missed me?" he asked in a husky voice.

"I've been busy," she said, evading a direct answer.

"At night, perhaps? Have you lain awake thinking of us?"

"Have you?" she countered. She went very still, as if she had felt the earth shake and was waiting for another tremor.

"Yes." His answer was immediate and unequivocal. "I've made Thomas the administrative manager of the Downs. Between him and the foreman, things should run smoothly enough. If there's any differences, they can come to Dad or me."

"That sounds practical," she said, confused by the change of topic.

"Yes. We've sold off a large part of the sheep and moved the rest to the station in New South Wales. We have a good man in charge there, too. The gold mine is doing well."

"Must be nice to have the Midas touch," she managed to quip with a show of her old spirit.

"Well," he said modestly, "actually, it isn't large, but it produces regularly."

"And the experimental station?"

"That's coming along, too."

She drew a careful breath and tried to feel nonchalant about his presence. "Sounds like your life is in order."

"Only the business part. My personal life is in one hell of a mess."

She was startled by his declaration. Her eyes were captured by his. The teasing had gone, and he was serious now, she saw. Her fingers plucked nervously at her skirt, and she forced them to stop, afraid that any action on her part would give away the rapid beating of her heart.

Had he fallen in love with Emerald? Was the problem that she didn't love him in return? That idea had never occurred to Kim. When she had sent Emerald to him, she had assumed the young woman would fall for Sean immediately. Any female in her right mind would. And Emerald was very intelligent.

"How is Emerald?" she asked. She may as well get it all out in the open, she decided, taking charge of the conversation.

"Fine. She's a lovely creature. Gentle. Kind. A delight to be around."

Kim nodded. She wanted him to be happy—of course she did—but hearing his words of praise hurt in unexpected places, like from the top of her head to the bottom of her toes. She wanted him to state his business, then leave.

"I knew you'd . . . like her," she managed.

"She's like a delicate piece of porcelain," he continued, "exquisite, but not the type that appeals to me."

Kim was shocked into silence. She couldn't think of a word to say. "Wh-why?" she finally stuttered.

He wondered if she would believe him after all the months in which he had taunted her, calling her General and sardonically letting her know he didn't care for her independent ways. He knew he would have to proceed cautiously if he was going to convince her of his sincerity.

"I like a woman who is more, shall we say... dynamic? Perhaps unpredictable is the word," he mused, sliding his fingers through her curls and arranging the strands smoothly about her shoulders. He carefully placed one dark lock near her breast and forced himself away from that delectable treat. There was much to be said before he took her into his arms. He wanted her to be sure, of herself and of him, before he made love to her again.

Kim felt as if fire ran through her skin at his gentle touch. She gave her hair a toss over her shoulder. "I thought she would be perfect for you."

"I know you did. It was generous of you to send her to me."

A flush spread slowly up her face. So he had realized that. She darted a glance in his direction. He didn't seem angry.

He shifted, and suddenly his shoulder was pressing hers. Unable to help himself, he dropped his arm around her and pulled her close. "But then, I've known for a long time how generous you are."

She tried to stand, to get away from him, but his embrace tightened, drawing her closer. "Let me go, please."

"Never," he replied. His lips touched her temple while his hand slipped across her waist to caress her side.

"Sean," she said repressively.

"Kiss me," he murmured, trying to find her elusive lips. His need for her was a flame that engulfed his senses. He only knew how much he wanted her. And how long it had been since he had held her. "You've driven me mad, given me nothing but trouble for months—"

"I've given you trouble!" she said indignantly, her voice going up in volume as anger grew in her. He was not going to barge in and treat her like some convenient amusement. She caught his hand that was wandering erotically over her abdomen and down onto her thighs. "You can't pop in here out of the blue and expect me to . . . to *entertain* you for the odd weekend or so whenever you're in town. Do you hear me?"

"Yes," he breathed, nuzzling along the side of her face.

"I'm not going to have an affair with you." She sounded decisive, but inside she wasn't so sure. If he kept this up . . .

"Right."

"What's wrong with Emerald? Why aren't you making love to her?" She waited anxiously for the answer.

"Because I don't want to. There's only one woman I want. That's you. It's you I love."

His hands lifted her and put her down in his lap. With one hand he unzipped her boots and removed them, putting her feet on the sofa and turning her so that he could hold her against his chest.

"You don't," she denied. "Emerald—"

His eyes blazed as he glared at her. "When I want a woman, I'll go get her. You don't have to send one to me."

"Well, you weren't doing so great," she scoffed, her own temper coming to her rescue. She wedged her hands between them and tried to push herself off him. "Besides, she was perfect, absolutely perfect!" she heatedly defended her choice.

He merely looked at her.

"She was!"

He shook his head, and the firelight picked out the embers in his hair. Kim fought an urge to bury her fingers in the smooth flames. She was acutely aware of his hard thighs under hers and the pounding of his heart beneath her hands.

"Perfect for some man, maybe, but not for me," he thundered at her. "How can you be so thickheaded?" he added insultingly.

This seemed to be escalating into a full-blown quarrel. She took a calming breath and tried to reason with him. "Sean, I think you've gotten confused by this thing between us."

"It's passion between us, not a thing," he corrected with a dangerous narrowing of his eyes. "I'll show you."

"No," she gasped as his arms brought her inexorably closer. His lips settled on her throat and left a burning inferno of desire there. His hand slid under her sweater and found her breast. He caressed her until she was breathless with longing.

"Tell me that you want me," he demanded hoarsely. "I've given you all the time I can. Now tell me you missed me as much as I've missed you. When you left, at first I was furious that you had turned down my proposal; later there was only the loneliness."

"Of course you were angry, but I knew there wasn't a chance of marriage working between us," she explained miserably.

"Shut up," he ordered. "You don't know anything at all."

"Don't tell me to shut up. I don't like it." She set her lips stubbornly together and wouldn't give in to the storm he was creating with his magic touch.

His lips brushed across hers. "Do you have any idea how much I need you? I need to touch you and hold you and make love to you. I like to tease you and argue with you and discuss business with you. I like falling asleep with you in my arms and waking up the same way in the morning."

"Don't," she whispered shakily, suddenly close to tears.

"And you need me," he murmured as if this fact negated all her arguments. "When you get sick."

Closing her eyes, she tried to calm her whirling senses. "I don't get sick. I take a pill for that."

"Yes, but when you have morning sickness, you'll need me to help you then and to carry you back to bed," he said softly, his hands warm and gentle, cupping her stomach as if he could already feel the child growing there.

"Morning sickness," she repeated blankly. She had never allowed herself to think of having children with him.

"You will need me then, won't you?" he asked. All traces of teasing left his voice, and she realized he wasn't playing games with her. "Marry me, Kim."

"What if you find your sweet, yielding woman and you're already married to me?" she demanded. "What then?"

"I hurt you with those thoughtless words, didn't I? And you, with your generous heart, sent me the woman you thought I'd love, but I didn't fall in love with Emerald, Kim, just as I didn't love Mary. I admire and like them both, but I don't love them. I never had such a passion for another woman that all I could think of was carrying her off to some private place and making mad love to her every single time I saw her." He fell silent and waited.

She slipped her hands up his shoulders. "I have missed you," she confessed, her heart beating irregularly.

His brow furrowed earnestly as he sought the words to convince her. "We can make a marriage work. You're wonderful at organizing your time, and I've got things under control at the station now. We can arrange to be wherever we're needed. If we can't, then we'll weather the separations."

She gazed into his eyes and saw his sincerity, his deep faith in both of them. Did he really love her? He hadn't the first time he proposed. She was sure of it.

He cupped her face in his hands. "When you sent Emerald, I realized how totally I loved you. I hoped it meant you loved me, that you loved me enough to want my happiness above all else."

She looked down, embarrassed that he had read her intentions so easily.

His thumbs rubbed over her lips. "I was afraid, though. I mean, you usually go after what you want—"

"I couldn't. I was afraid, too. I thought this attraction between us was temporary, but when I realized I loved you—"

"When?" he demanded. "When did you know you loved me?"

"When I called you."

He closed his eyes. "All that time wasted. I loved you then, too. I just didn't know it." He opened his eyes to glare at her. "All I knew was that I could hardly concentrate on what Thomas was telling me about the station, I was so aware of you."

"Do you love me? Truly? Be sure, Sean," she pleaded, her heart in her eyes. "I couldn't bear it if this was only desire that would burn out with time."

"I'm sure. When Emerald arrived, I was so angry with you for refusing my proposal that I decided she would make the perfect wife, but realizing that, I knew that's what you thought, too. And then I knew you loved me . . . and that I loved you," he explained patiently. "I waited to come to you because I didn't want passion to get in the way." He buried his fingers in her hair and brought her face close to his. "I want more than that. I want your love, your commitment to me and our future. I want children and grandchildren. I want to grow old with you and to lie next to you in a tiny churchyard way out in the back of beyond for all eternity. Marriage, Kim. That's the way it will have to be."

He breathed deeply, holding back the strength that wanted to crush her to him and demand that she answer. Why wasn't she answering? For a second he knew the agony of failure. He had been wrong. She didn't care that much for him.

And then he realized she couldn't answer. She was crying. Pressing her face against him, she wept in choking sobs that shook her body like a winter wind.

"Kim," he said in deep tones. "Kim, my love."

Her arms circled his neck, and she held on to him, unable to stop the overflowing of emotions kept too tightly reined for days and weeks and months.

"You're crying because you're so happy, right? Just nod your head, so I can stop worrying," he requested gently, a hint of laughter invading his voice.

"Yes," she sobbed. "Yes, I'm happy. I love you. I thought you would be married to Emerald by now. I saw you making love to her."

He looked rather startled. "That's impossible. I never touched the woman. Except for a kiss or two," he added in all honesty. "But that was because I was mad at you. I did *not* make love to her."

"I meant in my imagination. Oh, Sean, I thought I would die." She raised her face to him, and he saw the misery she had lived with.

"You crazy, sweet, loving, little dummy." The tenderness he had felt once before for her rushed over him, overpowering him with the need to protect and cherish her. He also needed to make love to her. "I need you. Now. This minute."

"Yes," she said, answering all his questions with the word.

Lifting her into his arms, he carried her down the short hallway. In her bedroom their clothes seemed to float away, and soon they stood as they once had by a rain-swollen stream, each gazing at the perfection of the other.

"I've never known a more beautiful woman," he told her, urging her into bed and lying beside her. His hand caressed her throat, her breasts, her thighs. He explored all of her with the most patient gentleness she had ever known. It brought tears to her eyes again. "What is it, love?"

"You make me feel so loved. I've been restless, something was missing from my life, but I didn't know what. I thought I could work and get over you."

"It didn't happen, did it?" His smile was one of supreme satisfaction. "I couldn't forget you, either. After our night in France I was haunted. I knew I was going to have to come to you. That's why I was already in Australia when you called about my father."

Her eyes opened wide. "Sean!"

He leaned over her and kissed each rosy nipple. "I wasn't going to confess that," he admitted. "I don't want you to get the idea that you can lead me around by the nose."

She laughed at the thought, and his deep chuckle joined in. "Volcanoes can't be led. They just sit there and blow their tops, don't they?"

His mouth descended toward hers. "If I don't have you soon, I'm definitely going to explode," he warned. He curled his fingers through her hair. "It seems I've waited a lifetime to find you, but now you're mine. You may not be the perfect woman, my love, but you're perfect for me." He laughed softly as if he found the thought very amusing.

For a second she was tempted to tease him and question what parts of her he considered less than perfect, but she realized it didn't matter. He loved all of her, totally and endlessly...just as she loved him. With a sigh she burrowed deeper into his arms and felt his warmth surrounding her. It would be fun living in the heart of a volcano.

CARLA NEGGERS CAPTIVATED YOU ONCE—AND SHE'LL DO IT AGAIN

Trade Secrets, Temptation #162, introduced you to one unique Killibrew sister, Juniper. Juniper's dedication to the family business was hardly rewarded—Cal Gilliam, millionaire rogue, snatched the firm right out from under her and forced her to go nose-to-nose with him in combat. No one, however, *made* her fall head over heels in love with the man.

Now in Temptation #190, *Family Matters*, Juniper's strong-minded sister, Sage Killibrew, encounters yet another rogue. It all begins with an urgent telegram from her long-lost grandfather, which lands Sage in hot water not only with her relative but also with the hero and the hero's father! Sage and *her* rogue, Jackson Kirk, have a few family matters to settle before they can stop the feuding and start the loving. . . .

Look for Temptation #190, *Family Matters*. Destined to captivate you in February!

TEMPJ-1

COMING NEXT MONTH

#193 SPIRIT OF LOVE JoAnn Ross

When a handsome stranger tried to convince Justine that he'd been dreaming of her for months, she was highly skeptical. But the more she saw of Colin, the easier it was to picture herself haunting him in the wee hours....

#194 THE NESTING INSTINCT Corey Keaton

Grey Powell might have outbid Megan Sinclair on the house she desperately wanted, but the heirloom hidden inside would be hers! Much to her surprise, Grey willingly gave her access to the house...and anything else she cared to explore.

#195 MORE THAN WORDS Elizabeth Glenn

Lee Ann Chung was at her wits' end with her hopelessly unruly dog, Doofus, so she enrolled him in obedience school. There she met the star canine, but it was his master who exuded a rare brand of animal magnetism....

#196 OVER THE RAINBOW Sandra Lee

After a storm brought Hal into Dana's life, she thought clear skies were finally coming her way. But dreaming of a future with him, she realized, was like chasing rainbows....

MAIL-IN-OFFER

OFFER CERTIFICATE

I have enclosed the required number of proofs of purchase from any specially marked "Gifts From The Heart" Harlequin romance book, plus cash register receipts and a check or money order payable to Harlequin Gifts From The Heart Offer, to cover postage and handling.

002

CHECK ONE	ITEM	# OF PROOFS OF PURCHASE	POSTAGE & HANDLING FEE
	01 Brass Picture Frame	2	$ 1.00
	02 Heart-Shaped Candle Holders with Candles	3	$ 1.00
	03 Heart-Shaped Keepsake Box	4	$ 1.00
	04 Gold-Plated Heart Pendant	5	$ 1.00
	05 Collectors' Doll Limited quantities available	12	$ 2.75

NAME ______________________________

STREET ADDRESS ____________________ APT. # _____

CITY _______________ STATE _______ ZIP _______

Mail this certificate, designated number of proofs of purchase (inside back page) and check or money order for postage and handling to:

Gifts From The Heart, P.O. Box 4814
Reidsville, N. Carolina 27322-4814

NOTE THIS IMPORTANT OFFER'S TERMS

Requests must be postmarked by May 31, 1988. Only proofs of purchase from specially marked "Gifts From The Heart" Harlequin books will be accepted. This certificate plus cash register receipts and a check or money order to cover postage and handling must accompany your request and may not be reproduced in any manner. Offer void where prohibited, taxed or restricted by law. LIMIT ONE REQUEST PER NAME, FAMILY, GROUP, ORGANIZATION OR ADDRESS. Please allow up to 8 weeks after receipt of order for shipment. Offer only good in the U.S.A. Hurry—Limited quantities of collectors' doll available. Collectors' dolls will be mailed to first 15,000 qualifying submitters. All other submitters will receive 12 free previously unpublished Harlequin books and a postage & handling refund.

OFFER-1RR